S0-BBH-020

Neonatal Nurses

Sisters who save lives!

Sisters Penny and Alice love working together in the Newborn Intensive Care Unit at Washington's Wald Children's Hospital. Treating the hospital's newest arrivals, Penny and Alice dedicate their days and nights to their young patients. But is it time that somebody dedicated their time to Penny and Alice, too? Perhaps surgeon Benedict and doctor Dougie might be just the men to heal their neglected hearts!

Step into the world of these neonatal nurses with…

A Nurse to Claim His Heart by Juliette Hyland

Neonatal Doc on Her Doorstep by Scarlet Wilson

Available now!

Dear Reader,

As a romance reader, I have always loved series and duets. They are some of my favorite things and getting to write my first one with the amazing Scarlet Wilson was a legit dream come true. I think I only fangirled a little on our Zoom call!

When Scarlet suggested writing sisters, I was so excited. Penny's relationship with her sister, Alice, mirrors a bit of my relationship with my sister. We are always there for each other but also the first to call the other out when something needs to be said. In fact, she helped with the idea this book started with by saying that my heroine needed a palate cleanser after her cheating ex. And from that giggly conversation, a fake relationship with the hospital playboy was born!

Dr. Benedict Denbar is one of my favorite heroes! A man who loves his patients, works hard, but doesn't get close to anyone. Until Penny marches into his life and forces him to question everything. Penny is his match, the woman he's meant to be with. Now, if only they can get over their past hurts to find their future.

Juliette

A NURSE TO CLAIM
HIS HEART

—————

JULIETTE HYLAND

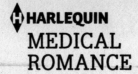

HARLEQUIN

MEDICAL
ROMANCE

If you purchased this book without a cover you should be aware
that this book is stolen property. It was reported as "unsold and
destroyed" to the publisher, and neither the author nor the
publisher has received any payment for this "stripped book."

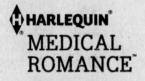

HARLEQUIN®
MEDICAL
ROMANCE™

Recycling programs
for this product may
not exist in your area.

ISBN-13: 978-1-335-40917-1

A Nurse to Claim His Heart

Copyright © 2022 by Juliette Hyland

All rights reserved. No part of this book may be used or reproduced in
any manner whatsoever without written permission except in the case of
brief quotations embodied in critical articles and reviews.

This is a work of fiction. Names, characters, places and incidents
are either the product of the author's imagination or are used fictitiously.
Any resemblance to actual persons, living or dead, businesses,
companies, events or locales is entirely coincidental.

This edition published by arrangement with Harlequin Books S.A.

For questions and comments about the quality of this book,
please contact us at CustomerService@Harlequin.com.

Harlequin Enterprises ULC
22 Adelaide St. West, 41st Floor
Toronto, Ontario M5H 4E3, Canada
www.Harlequin.com

Printed in U.S.A.

Juliette Hyland began crafting heroes and heroines in high school. She lives in Ohio with her Prince Charming, who has patiently listened to many rants regarding characters failing to follow the outline. When not working on fun and flirty happily-ever-afters, Juliette can be found spending time with her beautiful daughters, giant dogs or sewing uneven stitches with her sewing machine.

Books by Juliette Hyland

Harlequin Medical Romance

Unlocking the Ex-Army Doc's Heart
Falling Again for the Single Dad
A Stolen Kiss with the Midwife
The Pediatrician's Twin Bombshell
Reawakened at the South Pole

Visit the Author Profile page at Harlequin.com.

For Dad, whose bookshelf I longed to join as a kid.
Thanks for all the support and love.

**Praise for
Juliette Hyland**

"A delightful second chance on love with intriguing characters, powerful back stories and tantalizing chemistry! Juliette Hyland quickly catches her reader's attention…. I really enjoyed their story! I highly recommend this book…. The story line has a medical setting with a whole lot of feels in the mix!"
—*Goodreads* on *Falling Again for the Single Dad*

CHAPTER ONE

CROSSING HIS ARMS, Dr. Benedict Denbar played the "can I get comfortable in the small metro seat?" game. He considered standing, but it was early in the morning, and he was going to be on his feet all day while working at Wald Children's Hospital. At least the uncomfortable plastic let him avoid the crush of people pressed into the metro car. It wasn't much in the way of quiet time before his shift started, but it let him clear his head before starting the day as the attending physician in the level four neonatal intensive care unit.

The NICU was quiet. In fact the doctors and nurses did their best to keep the noise level below forty-five decibels as recommended by the American Academy of Pediatrics to protect the tiny babies in the unit. But the quiet wasn't restorative and the stress of the environment, where patients shifted from stable to critical in hours, sometimes minutes, wore on many of his colleagues. He'd seen dozens of doctors and nurses seek different specialties.

And he didn't blame them. But the NICU was his calling. His place to make a difference. His place to make amends.

He closed his eyes as his thoughts wandered to Olivia. They'd traveled there so often lately, as his dream of a high-risk maternity unit in the children's hospital was finally becoming a reality. Assuming Wald's Children's Hospital could fund the multimillion-dollar investment.

He'd been on the committee suggesting fundraising ideas, and there were several high-profile fundraisers planned. But was it enough?

He blew out a breath. This was his dream. Benedict needed the unit funded. Needed to find a way to support the mothers of the babies in his unit.

Medical care for NICU patients had come a long way since he'd stood over Olivia's incubator, not knowing that the heated crib was actually called an isolette. But too many mothers were separated from their children while they received care and their children were treated in the high-risk nursery.

If only she'd been born a few weeks later… a few days even. If the world were fair, he'd be helping plan her eighteenth birthday now. But life wasn't fair.

And if she'd lived, he wouldn't be sitting on an uncomfortable chair in DC. Hell, he probably wouldn't have become a physician…at least not a pediatrician specializing in neonatal care. His life would look completely different.

All sacrifices he'd have gladly made to raise Isiah's daughter. His brother had been gone for nineteen years this month. Nineteen years… A lifetime.

He'd now lived more of his life without his baby brother than with him, but Benedict still found himself searching for him. Still longed to call him at the end of the day. It was a funny feeling to miss part of yourself.

Benedict shook himself and straightened in his seat. He'd thought of Isiah a lot over the last few months. And Olivia, and her mother, Amber— his wife.

At least his wife according to legal documents. A connection bonded by a vow he'd made to Isiah, but never even sealed with a kiss. A vow that shouldn't have been necessary, if Isiah had only listened to Benedict's arguments about his shift from certified drag racing to illegal street racing for cash.

Amber had arrived at his door less than two weeks after Isiah's funeral. Tears streaking across her face as she protectively cradled her belly. He'd known her predicament and that her mother would disown her for getting pregnant at eighteen. An unwed mother would not be welcome in her home. It might have been the twenty-first century, but that didn't matter.

Isiah had planned to use the winnings of his last illegal street race to run away with her. If only he'd told Benedict, they'd have found a different way.

There was almost always a different way. Something else you could try. But that was a lesson that came with age and experience. And blinded by love, his brother hadn't been able to think clearly.

His phone dinged, and he pulled it from his pocket. His mother's face with a new ring held in front of her face and giant smile with a guy he did not recognize flashed on his screen. He couldn't stop his eyes from rolling to the ceiling. If she made it to the altar, this would be her sixth husband, and he'd lost count of the number of fiancé's she'd dumped or been dumped by. Yet, with each new relationship, she sent him a text…that he never answered.

Love.

Benedict scoffed and ignored the stare from the elderly woman sitting next to him. He hadn't meant to let noise out, but love or the feeling that people claimed was love really was too fallible to be trusted. It either turned to hate or destroyed.

Responsibility, friendship, even honor, last longer than love. Which was why he'd stepped in where his brother could not. Accepting a platonic union as they'd helped each other mourn the loss of his brother and then the loss of Olivia when she was born too early.

So tiny.

And with that, his connection to Amber should have ended, and in many ways it had. They'd married when he was nineteen, and separated three days before he'd turned twenty-one, just after he'd enrolled at Oregon State University, determined to help babies like Olivia.

But Amber hadn't wanted the shame of a divorce. Her family, difficult though they were, were all she had left now that Isiah and Olivia were gone. She'd asked him to stay married, at least on paper. And he'd agreed, after all he'd promised till death, and Benedict hadn't wanted to follow down his parents' path of broken vows. He'd meant the words when he said them—vows were not to be made lightly no matter what his mother and father thought of their promises.

So they'd stayed married. Amber got to keep the illusion that she was married for her mother and Benedict got to do right by the woman his brother had loved. It wasn't as though he'd ever planned to marry for love anyway. He'd seen how dangerous that was, so what did it matter if he remained married to Amber for duty's sake?

A young couple entered the metro with a newborn. The young man wrapped his arms around the mother. They looked exhausted, but most parents at that stage wore exhaustion well, almost basked in it as they loved on their baby. The woman laid her head against her partner's shoulder while cradling the infant wrapped against her chest. It was picture perfect, but one never knew what went on in other people's homes.

He deleted the text from his mother, then looked at the message he'd sent Amber yesterday about starting their divorce procedures. She'd left it on Read. He shook his head as he added following up with her to his mental to-do list. A few weeks ago, she'd asked to wait a bit longer while she dealt with her mother's illness.

But how long?

The metro slowed, and Benedict leaned forward as the door to the Foggy Bottom Station opened. Penelope Greene, Penny, stepped onto the train. She met his gaze, nodded and quickly shuffled to the other side of the car.

He tried not to let that hurt.

He and Penny were colleagues. Nothing more. Though seven years ago, they'd been as close as work colleagues could be. Coffee breaks, laughter and support as she found her way as a junior nurse, and he navigated the last days of his residency. He'd been attracted to her, desperately so. Their friendship nested on the edge of so much more. He'd dreamed of kissing her more often than he cared to remember.

But Penny had made no secret of the fact that she wanted a family. A re-creation of the happy home that she and her little sister, Alice, had grown up in.

For a brief second all those years ago, Benedict had wished he could give her those things. Wished that he believed a happily-ever-after was possible. Wished he were free to promise things that no one could really promise. Life shifted too unpredictably for anyone to truly promise for better or worse and forever.

And love eventually faded…if you were lucky. If you weren't, it destroyed you, body and soul.

And Penny was an unfortunate exhibit in that truth. She'd been engaged when she left Wald Children's Hospital three years ago. He'd tried to be happy for her. Tried to ignore the tingle of jealousy that crested through him. And he'd tried not to be happy when she'd returned last year.

She'd moved back in with her sister, another nurse in the NICU. The fancy ring on her left hand gone, though the tan line had been visible through most of the winter. She didn't smile as much as she had before. There were no flirtatious jokes or coffee runs anymore. But it wasn't Benedict's place to ask what had happened.

It was selfish to wish they could go back to their friendly talks. Selfish to be glad she was back…without a wedding band. But he was glad, so glad.

The metro car jerked and halted as the lights turned off. A few cries of alarm echoed in the car before the emergency lights flipped on.

"You've got to be kidding me." The words of the passenger next to him floated into the metro car, and Benedict involuntarily nodded.

The DC metro usually ran without a hitch. But with over six hundred thousand daily commuters and tourists, when slowdowns occurred they affected nearly every sector of the city, from government and military employees to private-sector employees and medical providers to the tourists who crammed in each day to see the National Mall and free museums.

"No!" the young mother he'd seen earlier shouted as she gripped her baby. "Is there a doctor, please?"

Benedict stood and moved toward the couple, and he saw Penny start toward them too.

"What's wrong?" Benedict couldn't see anything immediately wrong with the child, but the lighting wasn't great.

Penny grabbed her cell phone and turned on the flashlight function.

Benedict nodded to her and redirected his attention to the mother. "I'm Dr. Denbar, a neonatal pediatrician, and this is Penny Greene, one of the finest NICU nurses you will ever meet. What is going on?"

"My brother has seizures." She choked out as her partner patted her knee. "Last night Cole jerked forward. I remember my brother doing that. But it was over so quick. I thought. But just now he stiffened again. Our pediatrician recommended we go to Wald Children's this morning, to be evaluated in the ER."

"Can we get a little more light in here, please?" Penny called as she looked to the four closest riders. "You can stay where you are, but if you have a cell phone and could turn on the flashlight, that would be helpful."

A few passengers followed her instructions, but he saw several others hold up their cells without adding their flashlight. No doubt filming the encounter.

Why was everything a social media post?

"Does anybody have a towel?" Benedict asked, not really expecting an answer. The Blue Line that they were on was usually trafficked by commuters at this hour. When no one immediately volunteered, Benedict racked his brain, trying to think of something the train full of commuters would have.

"Can I please have your BDU shirt?" Penny's question sounded more like an order as she addressed the military member to her right. "It will provide the baby some safety as we evaluate him. The floor here is the definition of unsanitary."

The military sergeant quickly unbuttoned the outer layer of his battle uniform and handed it to Penny. She handed him her phone, and he stood with the light over the area. She was a commanding presence in the NICU and out.

Laying the uniform on the floor, she looked at the mom. "Can we take a look at your son?"

The mother carefully unwrapped the child and gingerly handed him to Benedict. The baby looked to be about six weeks old. Given the size of the newborns Benedict routinely worked with, this guy was hefty—which was perfect.

Until the left side of his body tightened. He saw Penny look to the watch on her wrist as she timed the muscle group tensing. It was classic myoclonic seizure presentation in an infant. Something most parents wouldn't recognize, unless they had a family member that experienced seizures.

"Forty-three seconds," Penny stated as the muscles released.

"Call the train operator. Then alert the NICU

that we have a patient inbound and ask to have the neurologist on call notified."

Penny nodded as she moved toward the call station behind him.

"You were right to head to Wald Children's this morning. And I think your son is having myoclonic seizures."

The boy's limbs seized again, and Benedict felt his insides twist. So little and three seizures in less than five minutes. Seizure clusters were not uncommon, but he wanted this little guy somewhere where he had access to medical equipment.

"The cars separated behind us. The metro may be stuck for at least an hour—"

"We can't wait that long. He seized again while you were talking to the conductor." Benedict felt bad for interrupting, but at least an hour likely meant at least three to get them back on their way. And there were still three additional stops before they reached theirs, then Wald's was another ten-minute walk. A very pleasant commute, when you didn't have an ill child.

"I know." Penny turned her attention to the parents. "I already worked out with the conductor for Dr. Denbar and I, and one of you to walk along the emergency route back to Foggy Bottom Station. An ambulance will meet us there to transport us to Wald's."

Of course she'd worked it out. Penny and her sister, Alice, had grown up all over the place as their parents, both active duty military, had moved around the world. The girls were two of the most resourceful women he'd ever met. And bound tightly together after a childhood of picking up and leaving everything but family behind.

Alice still kept her distance from him. She was professional in the hospital but reserved. If he'd had more than a workplace friendship with Penny, he might have suspected Alice hated him for breaking her sister's heart. But their connection hadn't been that deep—though it had felt like it could be. *So easily.*

Shifts where one or both Greene sisters were on duty ran smoother than any he'd ever experienced.

"It has to be me." The mom pursed her lips as she looked at her partner. "I'm breastfeeding and…"

"I know." Her partner leaned his head against hers before kissing it. "I'll be there as soon as I can. Promise." Then he met Benedict's gaze. "My heart and soul are going with you. Take care of them."

"Of course," Benedict answered, trying to ignore the push of emotions deep in his soul. Emotions that he'd been able to ignore until recently.

Until Penny returned, if he were honest.

The look of love between the two sent a pang of jealousy through him. No one had ever looked at him that way, and he never expected anyone to. But a tiny ache in his heart pressed against him.

"I think it will be best if you wrap him next to you again. The emergency evacuation route is tight." Penny gently bent to pick up Cole. She cradled him while his mother readjusted the wrap, then smiled as she handed him over. "Such a handsome little man."

"He is." Her voice shook a little as she kissed the top of her baby's head and stood.

"Ready?" Benedict asked as he stood by the door. He'd never pulled the emergency exit on a metro car, never seen it pulled. It was not an experience he'd craved. Particularly with a sick baby.

"Ready or not, we're going." Penny's gaze wandered past his to Cole's mom. "I'll lead, you and Cole in the middle and Benedict... Dr. Denbar in the back. Okay?"

Benedict waited for Cole's mother to acknowledge the plan, then he pulled the emergency release button and pushed open the door. "I'm glad you were on my train this morning, Penny." The words weren't meant to come out, but he couldn't draw them back in now.

And he didn't want to. Benedict didn't know what to do with those thoughts, so he let them slide away as he watched Penny step into the dark tunnel.

A small boy started clapping as they left and soon the whole metro car was clapping. It was a weird and unique way to start his morning shift. One he hoped he never had to repeat.

Though he didn't mind starting the morning with Penny... He let that thought slide away too as he gripped the edge of the railing of the evacuation path. The tunnel was barely lit, not completely dark but close. He was thirty-eight years old and being afraid of the dark was ridiculous, but he'd never been able to banish the fear instilled by his parents' long punishments. The shadows pressing along the side sent worries draping through him. His feet shook as he made his way on the tight path. So he turned his gaze to the leader of their small pack.

Penny's shoulders were straight, her dark hair pulled into a ponytail. So in control of the uncontrollable. It sent a wave of calm through him. He couldn't put words to that either, but he didn't push the thought away this time. Penny was here and he was happy about it. That was enough for now. He'd figure out the emotions later, find a way to categorize them and move past them.

"Your actions today made the news." Alice flipped her laptop around on the kitchen counter with a grin as she held up her glass of wine and winked. "A spokesman for the hospital used it as an opportunity to raise the issues of fundraising for the new wing, since they couldn't comment on the child's condition and you and Dr. Denbar were unavailable for comment."

Penny rolled her eyes as she grabbed a frozen dinner from the freezer and popped it into the microwave. No one had asked them to give a statement, though she would have declined to comment. So it was probably for the best.

They'd been granted a reprieve, for now. But with the fundraising push for the expanded wing so they could offer maternal health support for high-risk pregnancies, she suspected she and Benedict would be trotted out to help with the public relations for the multimillion-dollar project.

Benedict likely wouldn't mind. The maternity wing was his brainchild.

She mentally wished she'd used her day off to meal prep, so she would have had a stash of leftovers in the fridge, as she watched the frozen meal spin in the microwave. But she'd spent the day out at the park, drawing and reading trivia books.

And trying not to think about today.

A year ago today, she'd sold her wedding dress. Sold it on the day she'd expected to tie the knot. Not that she should have expected to walk down the aisle. It had been the third date she and Mitchel had set.

Third date!

Who set three wedding dates? She hated how accommodating she'd been for the first two setbacks. How she'd bought each of his lies, let him smooth away all her worries.

Of course she wanted his mom, whom she'd never met because she was living abroad, to be at the wedding.

If she had a conflict, then rescheduling was the right move.

Her parents were willing to move mountains to be there for their daughters' special events. But not every parent put their child's needs and desires first. Mitchel had said it really mattered to him that she be there. So Penny had called the vendors and moved the date back.

The fact that she'd never met any of his family, even after offering to video call, bothered her. But she'd accepted his statements that his family wasn't close, but he hoped their family would be. The seemingly romantic statement was designed to placate her, and she'd swallowed it every time she'd worried something was off.

The second date had come and gone because he was starting a new job. As a business management consultant, he traveled all over, sometimes gone for three weeks a month. He claimed this new job would give him more time with her, and she'd fallen for that lie too.

Once again, Penny had waved away the sinking feelings in her stomach that something was wrong. She'd ignored the tiny voice screaming that something was off. She'd quieted her fear that he had cold feet. If only it had been so easy.

The third, and final, time she'd canceled everything was because his wife had sent her copies of their marriage certificate and pictures of their two little girls. She'd told her that she was welcome to the cheating bastard. Penny could still feel the embarrassment and shame from those angry missives.

So far from the fairy-tale ending she'd hoped for.

Not that she could blame the woman. Whether Penny had realized it or not, she'd been the other woman. The catalyst for a family breaking down. Objectively she knew Mitchel was completely to blame, but she'd overlooked so many red flags. She'd let him charm away all her worries because she wanted a family. Wanted to replicate the happy home life she and Alice had grown up in, but without having to pack up and leave every few years like when the US Army transferred her parents.

She'd agreed to move to Ohio for Mitchel,

but she'd made him promise that it was the only move they'd make, if they could help it. She'd spent her childhood packing her things, never getting too comfortable with friends because she'd have to leave.

She'd wanted a different life for her children. Wanted them to have friends from grade school that they still chatted with as adults. Wanted them to have the roots to a place they'd grown up in. And he'd agreed with her. Let her plan her dreams on his promises…promises that hadn't been worth anything. At least he'd suggested renting a townhome until they could find the perfect place—which of course never appeared.

It had made it easy-ish for her to move back to DC, to pick back up the life she'd had before. And none of her colleagues had pressed her about her return, or why her ring finger no longer held the fancy bauble Mitchel had purchased.

Fancy. She scoffed as the frozen dinner popped in the microwave. The brilliant diamond she'd showed off to all her friends had been a hunk of cubic zirconia. The pawnshop owner where she'd taken the last evidence of Mitchel's fraud took pity on her sob story and offered her sixty bucks.

And she'd taken it. Not because she needed the money, but because that was all she was going to get from the years of falsehoods she'd been fed. When she started dating again, she wasn't settling for less a second time. She'd get the fairy tale, or she'd move on. No more settling for Penny Greene.

"I'm not surprised people were filming, but it wasn't overly dramatic." Penny shrugged as she pulled the hot veggie lasagna from the microwave. "The baby is being evaluated for epilepsy. Given the family history, and the seizures Benedict and I witnessed today, I suspect that the diagnosis will come from neurology in a day or two. Hopefully they can find an anti-seizure med that helps."

"Benedict. Don't you mean Dr. Denbar?" Alice's tone rippled with a disgust that Penny didn't understand.

"We were friendly colleagues seven years ago, Alice." Penny lifted her wine glass, enjoying the light tang of citrus as it coated her tongue. Maybe cheap wine and a frozen dinner weren't the hallmark of the family life she'd thought she'd have by her thirties, but they did hit the spot after a long day.

"Friendly colleagues. Please, you had a huge crush on him, and he led you on, then jumped into bed with the next willing nurse or doctor to catch his eye." Her sister shook her head as she crossed her arms. "Playboy Denbar should come with a warning sign."

Penny raised her eyebrow as she met her sister's gaze. That nickname had not been assigned to Benedict when she'd met him, and she didn't think it appropriate now. Yes, the man dated a lot. But that was hardly a crime. He was young, intelligent and hot.

So hot! Just thinking of his soft dark eyes, full lips and toned body was enough to make her knees weak even now. The man was gorgeous. She'd wondered more than once if the world disappeared when he kissed you. Her fingers involuntarily touched her lips, but her sister didn't seem to notice.

Benedict was thoughtful, but a closed book. They'd had a great time at work, but Penny hadn't found out much about his past. Benedict had skirted around the standard "get to know you" questions. But she hadn't minded because they'd talked about everything else. Current affairs, movies, books, the never-ending traffic around DC and their favorite museums, over coffee and night shifts.

The friendship had never progressed outside the hospital, but she'd looked forward to seeing him each shift. Still looked forward to it, if she were honest. Though the woman that had returned to DC was a very different person than the one he'd joked with during their downtime.

Maybe he dated most of the eligible women in

the hospital, but he wasn't cruel. And he didn't love them and leave them. No, Benedict was up front. That was one thing he'd made sure everyone understood. He liked his solitary life—or claimed to.

On their late-night shifts, he'd seemed to waver in that belief. Or maybe that was just her heart forcing her brain to remember differently. Wishing that the man she'd seemed to have so much in common with also wanted the life she craved. But he hadn't…and time moved on. Even if her stomach still flipped every once in a while when she saw him.

Maybe she knew he always rode the third train on the Blue subway line when he was on shift at Wald Children's. And yes, it was a little upsetting that she was always a tad crestfallen on the days when the seat where he normally sat was empty. And maybe she'd considered asking if the seat next to him was taken this morning before chickening out…but only because they'd been friends once.

"We were close colleagues, or as close as closed-book Denbar gets, but he didn't want love, marriage and a family, and I do. He was honest and that is a quality severely lacking in some."

Her sister frowned, and Penny hated the look. It was Alice's fixing look. Not that anything in Penny's life needed fixing, but her sister on a mission was a force to be reckoned with. And Penny did not want to be her next project.

Alice was a little less than two years younger than her. They'd been best friends since Alice had learned to toddle after her. Bound together as their family had picked up and moved across the world.

"Say what you want but you pouted around this townhome for months, hoping he might ask you out." Alice huffed as she took a bite of her sandwich.

"I did not pout. At some point, the two of us really need to look into weekly meal planning so we aren't eating such pathetic dinners all the time." Penny stuck out her tongue before grabbing another bite of her frozen lasagna.

"Don't try to change the subject. And I am fine with my dinner. Thank you very much!" Alice took another bite of her sandwich and made sounds best suited to an over-the-top children's cartoon character pretending to enjoy a badly burned dinner his friend had cooked.

She swallowed, then looked directly at Penny, her blue eyes holding hers. "I know what today was supposed to be."

"It's a day like any other day." Penny shrugged, wishing it were the truth.

"So you don't miss Mitchel, the cheating scumbag who should rot for all eternity?"

Penny grinned. Her sister never just called her ex Mitchel, or her ex-fiancé. She always invented some provocative nickname that really got across just how much she hated the man. And if it didn't come out strong enough, Alice just kept adding until she felt there were enough derogatory terms to get her point across.

"No. I do not miss Mitchel." Penny took another sip of wine. She did *not* miss her ex, but she missed the idea of him. The idea of what their life together had seemed. She missed the life path she'd thought she'd been walking. And she hated how much she'd let Mitchel steal from her.

Not her money, though he'd taken plenty of that, always promising to pay his half for things like the move and household expenses. Then coming up short, claiming to have a bad sales month.

Must have been expensive to keep two homes.
Penny hated the bitter thought as it floated through her mind.

It wasn't the man she missed, but the woman she'd been, full of hope and trust. Of course that woman had gotten taken for a ride, so maybe it was a good thing she wasn't her anymore. She knew what she wanted, and she wouldn't settle for less. Her parents had found true love, and she could too. She just had to look and accept the warning signs if she saw them.

"I think you need a rebound." Alice opened the dating app on her phone, flipped it toward Penny and started scrolling through the images of eligible singles…or people claiming to be single.

Would she ever fully trust someone again? She wanted to. She really did.

Her heart flipped as her brain waffled. Her bed was lonely, and on nights when her shift in the NICU was overwhelming, she wished she had someone besides her sister to comfort her. To cradle her to sleep. Intimacy was so much more than a physical connection…though she missed that too.

"I'm not interested in a rebound, Alice." She laughed as an image of a man wearing a Mickey Mouse shirt, holding up a large fish with the caption I'm Your Catch, crossed her sister's phone's screen. "Does that image really work for picking up single woman?"

"We could ask?" Alice wiggled her finger toward the phone.

"Or we could swipe left!"

"Spoilsport." Alice playfully glared at her as she swiped left and held up the next potential match.

He was cute. The profile said he was a broker and into hiking. She looked over the profile, then shook her head. "Nope. He's not a dog person. Who doesn't like dogs?"

Alice looked at the picture, then shook her head. "He's adorable and it doesn't say he doesn't like dogs, just that he prefers cats. You can't look for perfect. Sometimes Mr. Right Now can become Mr. Right…assuming you aren't looking for a real Prince Charming. The secret prince only exists in those cheesy holiday movies we gobble up between Thanksgiving and Christmas every year."

Maybe fairy tales were rare, but they existed— she refused to give up that belief. But she didn't feel like arguing with her sister tonight.

"If you're so interested in the men on that app, maybe we should pick out your date for next Friday." Penny giggled, moving her finger toward the screen as her sister pulled the phone away.

"My dating life is quite healthy, thank you very much. But yours has been dismal since you moved back. You work, read trivia books, watch trivia shows, draw and go to bed. The repetition is even getting to me."

"I wasn't aware my love of trivia bothered you—or maybe it's that I always beat you." Penny chuckled as she held her wine glass in a mock toast to her sister.

"Stop changing the subject." She showed off another eligible bachelor. "The best way to get over someone is to get under someone else, you know." Alice winked as she held her phone up for Penny's inspection, but far enough away that she couldn't actually touch the screen. "He's cute."

The man on the screen was cute. Well built, with a deep smile and eyes that looked kind. But images were easy to fake. Still, as she looked at the smiling man, part of her yearned for a connection. Not with a stranger on a phone app, but a real connection.

Except people formed lasting connections via phone apps these days.

Her heart argued as the walls her brain had raised following Mitchel's betrayal wavered. She was lonely. A date that went wrong wouldn't be the end of the world.

But her confidence had been shattered. And she didn't know how to fix that. Why wasn't there a way for her to practice date? To get her feet wet, so to speak, without worrying about feelings getting tangled.

Ugh! her brain screamed. Pretend dating wasn't an option. She should just pick someone attractive and give it a whirl. So why was she hesitating?

She didn't have to make any choices tonight. "I think we should be discussing the movie we want to watch, not which men are hottest on your app."

"We can do both." Alice swiped right, then left as the images popped up on her phone. "It's fun."

"Alice!" she said before her lonely heart could force her walls down even further.

"Fine," her sister huffed in an indignation that only Alice could manage. "But if you don't want to spend every evening trying to convince Sooty to cuddle, you'll have to jump back in the dating pool at some point."

"At some point," Penny repeated. "But your cat is a good cuddle buddy. He might love me more than you now." Penny chuckled as the black cat slinked across the counter, nudged her wine glass, then glared at her as she pulled it out of the feline terror's reach. Sooty loved Alice, but the cat didn't care for anyone else, and he would never willingly cuddle with Penny.

No, her bed was solitary. But it didn't have to be… She could just swipe right on one of the apps she'd downloaded and never used. She glanced at her phone, pulled up a profile. A handsome man, her age, who claimed to be looking for real love. A Lasting Connection was the title of his profile. Her fingers hovered, then she swiped left.

Coward!

CHAPTER TWO

"I just worry that if we take her home, then something goes wrong. I... I... We've spent the last one hundred and fifty-seven days hoping, praying, yearning for Hannah to come home. Hoping she'd join the ranks of the NICU graduates. But now that the day is here, I worry we are rushing things. God, that makes me sound like such a terrible mother."

"No." Penny shook her head, making sure Natalie Killson was looking at her as she reinforced the message. "That does not make you a bad mom. It makes you a mother who spent over a hundred days here, watching and worrying. Excitement and fear do not cancel each other out and our brains are able to experience so many emotions at once."

Hannah giggled as she sat in her mother's lap, the tiny tubes that had been attached to her for months finally gone.

"That is the best sound ever." Benedict strode through the door, bent and smiled at Hannah.

The little one laughed again as her fingers reached for Benedict's nose. It took a bit longer for them to connect than an average five-month-old, but preemies took longer to hit their developmental milestones. Though Penny hoped that Hannah's hand-eye coordination would increase fast now that she was going home.

"You got my nose!" Benedict wiggled his face just a little, not enough to make Hannah lose her grip but enough to test her muscle control. The silly game made the baby smile again.

He was an excellent physician. Everyone talked about how he handled stressful situations. Always calm and coordinated to ensure their high-risk patients got the best chance at a normal life. But it was here that Penny thought he truly shined.

When the crisis was over. When their babies were ready to go home. When they were on the safe path, Benedict cooed over them, he played silly games—yes ones designed to help his assessments—but he enjoyed these moments. And that bedside manner was not something all physicians and nurses had.

Particularly in these units.

Treatment capability for preemies and micro-preemies, babies born weighing less than one pound twelve ounces or before twenty-six weeks gestation, had increased their survival rates. But this could still be one of the saddest and most stressful environments in any hospital. Many nurses and physicians kept themselves at a professional distance from the parents and patients to protect their mental health.

Penny understood the inclination. It let them do the best job they could for their patients—and that was what mattered most. But she'd never been able to maintain that blurred line. And neither had Benedict.

It was one of the things that had drawn her to him all those years ago. The reason she'd been so surprised when he'd announced on a late shift that he had no intention of having a family. Of being a father... Because a child should get the privilege of being loved by this man.

But he claimed not to want that. Claimed that he preferred his solitary life. Maybe all his love went to his patients? It was a nice, if lonely, sentiment. But Penny thought there was more to it. Tucked away in the past that he refused to discuss.

"Well, Ms. Hannah. We are going to miss you, but I am also so happy you are going home." Benedict tapped the child's knee, watching her eyes react to the movement, then stood. "She's come so far, Natalie. But we love to keep in touch with our babies. So don't feel like you can't reach back for questions…or to share important milestones."

Natalie's eyes teared up, and Penny passed her a tissue. Days like today were so exciting, and these looked like happy tears. The best kind.

"Thank you." She dabbed her eyes. "I remember the first day I walked through the doors here. The pictures of birthdays for the NICU graduates by the entrance gave me hope."

"That's what it's designed for." Benedict grinned, so proud of his wall of graduates.

"It's why Dr. Denbar petitioned for it to be put up." Penny pursed her lips as his dark eyes floated toward hers. He never boasted of his accomplishments, but Penny wanted Natalie to know that Benedict was the one who'd lobbied so hard for that addition. That his deep conviction in its necessity was what helped provide her peace.

He'd repeated to anyone that would listen that the NICU was scary. That it was the second to last place any parent planning to welcome a child wanted to be. She still remembered his words when the lead hospital human relations representative asked where the last place was. The nurses in attendance had all been stunned into silence, shocked the HR rep couldn't figure it out. But

Benedict had kept his eyes locked on the rep as he'd stated, *Planning final arrangements.*

The quiet words had carried over the buzz of electrical equipment and the representative had swallowed before writing a few notes in his electronic tablet. The hospital had approved the wall a week later, and Benedict had come in on his off day to help put it up. Then he'd carefully hung the pictures parents had sent him.

She'd seen more than one parent in distress staring at those images. Reaching for the hope they provided. Praying their babies got to join that wall.

"It's important to know this day can come."

Benedict looked at Hannah, but his eyes seemed far away. There was hurt deep inside him... She'd seen a touch of it years ago. But it radiated from him now before he shifted his position and the self-assured physician returned.

"Well, you are getting all the pictures of her!" Natalie let out a laugh, then a small sob as she nestled her head against her daughter's. "So many pictures." She kissed her cheek. "What else do we need to do?"

"Keep up with the appointments with her regular pediatrician and cardiologist. And Penny will give you her final discharge papers. And enjoy every moment." Benedict offered Hannah and then her mother one more smile, then he turned and met Penny's gaze.

His dark eyes seemed to touch a part of her that had been dormant for so long. Since those late nights in the on-call suite so long ago. A spark blazed between them, and she swallowed as she broke the connection first. This wasn't the time or place for her imagination to wander to unwelcome connections.

"After you finalize the discharge paperwork, can I speak with you for a moment, please?"

"Of course," Penny answered, hating the flutters in her belly. There was *no* need for that. She was just lonely. Clearly too lonely.

Then he was gone, and she was hoping her cheeks didn't look as hot as they felt. She looked at the list of instructions and pulled her thoughts back together. Hannah and her mother were what mattered now.

"For the most part, all you need to do is love on her. I know her cardiologist recommended you have a breathing monitor set up in her crib."

"I got it set up last week. It's set to the most sensitive setting. We won't miss anything." Natalie's fingers tightened just a bit on Hannah's midriff as she bent her head to kiss the child again.

Squatting so she was in line with Natalie, Penny made sure she was looking at her before continuing. "It doesn't need to be on the most sensitive setting. That will set off if she doesn't move in a few seconds. And that will happen nearly every night and make you worry. I promise setting it on the regular setting that the cardiologist suggested is more than enough."

"I… I just don't want to miss anything." Natalie's bottom lip shook as Penny patted her knee.

"I know. But life is going to get even more hectic now." She grinned at Hannah. "This little one will be walking and talking and keeping you on your toes. You need your rest too. Don't discount that.

"Do you have any other questions?" Penny asked as she stood and grabbed the discharge paperwork and passed it over.

"No." Natalie grinned as she stood and started putting Hannah in her car seat. "I'll probably think of twenty as soon as I hit the parking lot."

"Then just give us a call. The nurses' desk will answer anything you need. Hannah may be a NICU graduate as of today, but we are still here to help. Her pediatrician also has a twenty-four-hour nurses' line you can call." Penny grinned as Natalie lifted Hannah's car seat carrier. This was the best moment of her time here. The day she got to see the babies go home. See parents happy to return to a life outside the hospital.

"Thank you." Natalie wrapped her arms

through the car seat's handles and bit her bottom lip. "I really can't say thank you enough."

"No need to say thank you. But do send pictures. Bene... Dr. Denbar really does want them for his wall. Hanging them is one of his favorite activities."

Natalie took a deep breath, looked at her daughter and then the door. "Here we go."

Penny beamed as she watched the mother bounce toward the entrance. The happiest walk. A memory she filed away for a tough day. For a day when she needed the reminder that this outcome was possible. Each memory like this was a boost to her soul on those days when the world seemed unfair and dark.

"Penny?" Benedict...no, Dr. Denbar raised his hand as she exited the room.

Why did her brain refuse to think of him as anything besides Benedict? And why did her imagination insist on jumping to thoughts of them alone?

She could also deal without the musings on how he might kiss.

"I'm headed to the cafeteria for a cup of coffee. Care to join me?"

Her brain jumped at the idea of caffeine, but then it wavered. Coffee sounded lovely but she wasn't sure about going with Benedict. Her lonely soul was clearly reaching for connections.

And Benedict was an easy one. A path worn by an old friendship.

But he was also safe. He couldn't trick her into believing he wanted a family with her since she already knew he didn't want those things. Her heart was in no danger of getting attached.

It squeezed a little as she looked at the tall handsome man. *No danger*, she reminded herself.

"So we can discuss yesterday. HR reached out to me this morning, and I suspect they'll want to talk to you later."

"Oh." Penny nodded. Of course this was work-related. *As it should be.* The argument rattling around her brain didn't provide any comfort. "Sure. Though I don't know what HR would want from me. I can give a short statement, but we can't comment on the medical situation."

Benedict let out a low chuckle, and her stomach twisted as the luxurious noise enveloped her. It was a silly thing to hold on to, but Mitchel had rarely laughed. He'd argued that seriousness was the key to success. Though after finding out about his double life, Penny suspected he kept things as level as possible, so he didn't make a misstep and forget which partner had which inside joke.

The door to the elevator opened, and they stepped in. "You've never had to be part of a public relations campaign for a hospital trying to raise significant capital for a new project?"

"No." Penny shook her head. She kept herself inconspicuous whenever human resources went prowling for staff members to participate in their recruitment fairs and videos. But she'd seen Benedict in those videos, delivering his lines in a cool crisp tone.

His tall dark frame looking so elegant in his scrubs and a white lab coat. The perfect doctor image. Though a slightly fabricated one since no one wore lab coats anymore given the studies showing they were a repository for germs. Their babies couldn't afford any wayward germs sneaking in on lab coats, no matter how professional people thought they looked.

"I would have thought you and your sister would be prime targets. Sisters working at one of the top NICUs in the country. I mean the script practically writes itself." Benedict pushed the button for the lowest level and the elevator rattled as it started its descent.

Penny let out a soft laugh. "Alice has been involved, but I generally try to make myself scarce when they come combing for prospects." She didn't have a great reason for it. Alice had pressed her more than once to join her.

Service to others was one of the traits their parents had instilled in their girls. Penny and

Alice had each felt called to make a difference in the world. But in civilian careers. In fields where they weren't required to uproot their lives every three to five years.

"Well, our video made quite the stir in social media, and it was a slow news day, so it ran on the six and ten o'clock segments. And somewhere along the line, we became partners."

"Became…?" Penny's voice halted as the true meaning hit. "I see." His dark eyes held hers, and for just a moment she wished it were a true story. Her heart clenched again, and she barely caught the sigh trying to escape her throat.

Maybe she did need more company than Alice and her sister's grumpy cat. A quick rebound to dust off her dating game before she sought out happily-ever-after. "Is the hospital wanting us to clear it up? I mean colleagues date and there are more than a few married couples working here. It's not exactly scandalous."

"It's not a scandal they are worried about." Benedict gestured for her to exit first. "The story is better if we are a couple. That's all public relations campaigns are really. Stories."

Penny pinched the bridge of her nose. Yesterday they'd helped; that was the important thing. But Benedict was building to something, and she wasn't sure if the nerves twisting through her were warranted or not.

"And they are making a major push for a maternity suite for high-risk pregnancies. It's important that moms not be separated, if possible. Particularly because some of our cases don't go home. They…" He paused, swallowed, then continued. "They deserve all the time we can give them."

Again, Benedict's eyes seemed lost before he collected himself. Her hand itched to reach out to him. To provide comfort for the hurt she saw nestled there. But she didn't know what had caused it, and Benedict didn't seem inclined to elaborate.

Still, she wanted to reach him. To know more about the man than what he presented in the hospital. Such a dangerous desire. And one she didn't plan to give in to.

Penny agreed with the addition of the maternity unit. She'd seen women heartbroken because their babies had been rushed to Wald's while they recovered at separate hospitals. Sometimes they didn't make it to Wald Children's for almost a week. A lifetime. And it forced partners to divide their time between the mother of their child and their fragile newborns. No one should have to make that choice.

"All of that is true but I still don't understand what you're getting at."

"Two NICU professionals helping an infant on their morning commute is a good story. Two

NICU professionals who love each other *and* protect babies on their commute is a story that gets
a follow-up. That story gets the hospital a fun
story to tell for a topic that too often results in
tragedy."

She felt her lips fall open, but no words escaped.
*Was he really asking her to lie to HR? To
claim they were together...in love?*

He bit his lip before stepping up to the counter
and ordering his coffee. Then Benedict turned
and gestured to Penny. "Her coffee is on me."

Penny raised an eyebrow. "Benedict..."

"I insist, Penny. Please."

"Large blonde, two sugars and a splash of
cream, please." Penny nodded to the barista before turning her attention to Benedict. "So you
think coffee is a good bribe to get me to agree
to fake a relationship for a series of fundraising
events."

He at least had the good sense to look at his
shoes. "It's for a good cause."

"Sure, and the fact that Dr. Lioness is retir-
ing, and human resources has made no secret
of the fact that all interested internal candidates
should expect to attend these fundraising events,
isn't driving this request? Even a little?" She'd
heard Dr. Cooke, Dr. Webber and Dr. Garcia discussing the request last week. She and the other
nurses suspected the doctors were each trying

to feel each other out. Trying to determine who might be setting themselves apart with human resources for the head of the department.

If it was just about who was the best doctor, then the man handing her coffee would be the selectee. And everyone knew it. But this world rarely worked like that. Those with the best connections, those who proved they could network for the hospital, who could help raise money for research or facilities would get a leg up.

"I can't say that I don't want that position." Benedict shrugged. "I could help a lot of families."

Penny turned on her heel. She'd been in one fake relationship, one she hadn't known was fake. But still, she would not enter another.

"Penny!" Benedict chased after her as she pressed the button for the elevator. "Please." He sighed as they stepped into the elevator. "I need this maternity ward to work. And if us playing a bit of pretend helps that…"

"Why?"

"What?" Benedict's eyebrows knitted together as he met her gaze.

"*Why* do you need the maternity ward to be funded? It's important to you. I can tell that. And it's more than just it's a good idea that needs funding. It matters to you. So tell me the reason." She paused, then reiterated, "The real reason, unless it really is for the promotion boost. In which case, the answer is no."

Maybe it wasn't fair to press. She'd seen him shut down whenever she broached any topic that revolved around the life he'd had before starting work at Wald Children's. Dr. Benedict Denbar, amazing physician, hard worker, hot doctor... notoriously tight-lipped about anything personal.

"My brother's baby died a little less than twenty-four hours after she was born. Amber, her mother, never made it to the NICU. It...it nearly destroyed her." Benedict sighed. "I've never told anyone here that and I would appreciate..." The elevator shuddered and squealed as it came to a halt.

Penny let out a small cry as the car shook before dropping at least a flight and jerking to a stop. The lights flickered, then shut off completely.

Dear God. The darkness sank around him as Benedict felt his chest heave. As a kid, his parents had locked him and Isiah in a closet as punishment when they misbehaved, or when they tired of them, or just because. They'd hadn't always remembered to let them out.

That had made him uncomfortable in the dark. But he'd dealt with it, mostly.

Until the night Olivia passed.

Even all these years later, he could still remember the inky darkness followed by the squeal of machines until the hospital generator had kicked on. For a short time, he'd believed everything would be okay.

But exactly three hours and twenty-six minutes later, the generator failed. Olivia hadn't been able to survive the second interruption. With the medical training he had now, Benedict understood that Olivia likely wouldn't have survived much longer. But that didn't change the fact that she'd passed in the dark, without her mother.

By the time the kind nurse laid her on his chest, it was too late. So he'd held her and wept in the darkness. Wept for his brother, for the tiny life that hadn't gotten a chance and for her mother who'd never held her. It had taken another hour for the nurses to find enough flashlights to light the hallways and room. But by then his hatred, and fear, of the dark was cemented.

Rationally Benedict knew every room was the same whether the light was on or not, but his brain licked tendrils of fear down his spine whenever his eyes were unable to find a light source. Why hadn't the backup lights switched on? What had happened? When would the door open?

"Benedict?"

Penny's voice slid across the darkness and his chest lightened. He wasn't alone. Penny was here.

Penny.

He'd never spoken to anyone about those awful days following Olivia's passing. Even now they felt like a dream. Like they'd happened to someone else.

When he and Amber had returned to the tiny apartment they'd shared, Benedict had held her as she tried to process losing both her loves in less than six months. He wasn't Olivia's biological father, but he'd done his best to stand in for Isiah. He'd gone to as many appointments as possible, set up a crib and carried bags of clothes and supplies that Amber had purchased from garage sales to give her daughter the best chance, along with the tiny cartoon night-lights she'd purchased for the baby's room.

After Olivia was gone, they went through the motions of their "marriage of convenience" for as long as they could, but it felt hollow. Both Benedict and Amber were locked in their own private spheres of grief—for Isiah, for Olivia, for what could have been.

What should have been…

Amber had been as happy as he had when his acceptance to Oregon State had come through along with a full scholarship. But even now, all these years later, she wasn't interested in ending the union. All for family expectations… Amber's mother didn't mind her having an estranged husband, so long as she wore a ring on her hand.

For a long time, it had suited Benedict too not to face the idea of broken vows, and to keep that link to Isiah, however tenuous it was in reality, but something had changed in him lately.

Penny came back to the hospital.

Benedict tried to shake that thought out of his head but it persisted.

Came back without a ring on her finger. A second chance you never thought you'd have.

Nonsense, he told himself sternly. It was simply time to end a charade that had gone on for far too long.

"Benedict." Penny's hand traced along his jaw. "Breathe with me."

He heard her suck in air and loudly push it back out. Then she repeated the pattern. Benedict did his best to follow her breathing pattern and his heart started to slow. Until it realized that Penny's fingers were stroking his arms.

He knew it was a calming technique. One they used on the tiny infants in their isolettes so they knew they weren't alone. Penny's touch was light, but his body rejoiced at the simple touch.

How long had it been since someone touched him in such a way?

He dated, too often, at least according to some

of the whispers he'd overheard. But the touches of the women he dated weren't comforting. They satisfied a need, but when he was hurt, when he was scared, when his heart and brain rehashed past pain, he was alone. No comforting hugs, no soft commands to remember to breathe.

He was lonelier than he'd realized to be reacting to Penny's comfort like this. He didn't want the touches to end but relishing them wasn't a good option either. Reaching for her hand, Benedict gave it a gentle squeeze, then forced himself to let go. "I'm okay."

"Not sure that is the truth." Penny sighed into the dark. "Any idea what we do now?"

As if the universe was answering, the elevator phone rang into the pitch.

"I didn't know those still worked." Benedict let out a nervous chuckle as Penny's warmth evaporated as she started toward the phone. At least his eyes were starting to adjust to the darkness.

"It's federal law that all elevators built since the early 1990s have an emergency call button. Though it would be nice if I could see the button to push to answer."

Of course she would know about elevator codes. She used to spout trivia on long night shifts to help him stay awake. His local pub ran a trivia night every Tuesday and Thursday, and he always thought of her when he stopped in.

Had she ever been? Would she like to go with him?

Benedict filed those questions away. His brain was probably just trying to distract him from the dark. But the idea of spending time with Penny, even in these darkened conditions, sent a thrill through him. That should have terrified him. But he'd examine that feeling later…or perhaps not.

"Success!" Penny shouted as the crackle of the intercom echoed in the elevator. "Hello. This is Penny Greene. Dr. Denbar and I are in here. There are no patients with us."

"Straight to the point." Benedict sighed as he moved closer in case they needed to ask him any questions.

Penny's hip pushed against his, and he nearly lost his coffee cup. Though the brief connection would be worth a few stained scrubs.

"Good to know. This is Brian Hillion, firefighter with Engine Company Twenty-seven. Are there any injuries?"

"No," Penny responded, before letting out a nervous laugh. "Except my coffee cup. I dropped it when the elevator dropped."

"We'll get you another. I promise, Penny." The voice crackled through the intercom, and Benedict felt a twinge of something he feared was jealousy.

Which was ridiculous. To begin with, the firefighter was probably just trying to make her comfortable. And even if he was flirting with a discombobulated voice, Benedict had no claim on Penny.

Even if he was hoping she'd pretend to love him for a few weeks to benefit the hospital. No, he certainly didn't have a reason for the tingles of jealousy touching his soul.

"I need to hear from Dr. Denbar. Protocol."

"Here." He waited a minute before adding, "It's awful dark. I would have thought the backup lights would have come on."

"The cables snapped and the automatic brakes stopped the car. You're between floors. We'll get you out of the dark as soon as possible. Until then, hang tight. And, Penny, I'll make sure there's a coffee with a splash of cream and two sugars waiting when the door opens."

"Thanks."

"He knows your coffee order? Is that why you hesitated about faking a romance to help boost the fundraising?" The question was out before Benedict could fully process the words. For the first time in his memory, he was grateful for the darkness. At least he couldn't see the likely look of horror on Penny's face at such a rude set of questions.

"He dated Alice a while back." Penny words were crisp and he saw her outline move away.

He hated the distance she put between them but understood.

What had possessed his tongue?

"I am so sorry, Penny. That was beyond rude. I wish I could use hating the darkness as an excuse, but the truth is that was just plain old nosy and self-serving. I am truly sorry." He meant it too. There was no excuse for rudeness, and even less excuse for the evaporating jealousy. It should not make him happy that the man on the other end of the voice box hadn't dated the woman trapped with him.

Penny deserved to be happy. Deserved to find someone that wanted all the same things she did. He'd had a crush on her all those years ago, but it wouldn't have been fair to ask her out, knowing they wanted different things. He'd wanted her to get what she wanted. Still wanted it.

It hurt, more than he wanted to admit, to know that someone else would make her smile and laugh. Would get to see the flash of humor in her eyes when an interesting topic appeared. The woman had a bank of knowledge about so many things. From years of trivia study that she hoped would land her on her favorite quiz show. Then it had been canceled the year she turned twenty-one and was finally old enough to compete.

He'd dated many women but the things those women had enjoyed had exited his memory bank when the connection was severed. Yet Benedict had never forgotten the little things he'd learned through their friendship in those last years of his residency.

"I didn't immediately agree to deceive people because I do not enjoy lying. I've already..." Her breath hitched, and she coughed. "Lying is never the option."

"I could take you out." Another set of words slipped out of his mouth before he could fully process them. Except these ones he didn't really want to draw back in. Maybe it wasn't fair, but Benedict wanted to spend time with her. Wanted to see if her eyes still lit up when she was happy, if the crease just above her nose still appeared when she was thinking hard. Rekindle the friendship that had brought him so much joy.

"Then we wouldn't be lying. It could be real... sort of."

"You're asking me out? To help the hospital?" Penny sighed and he heard her slide down the wall.

Slowly making his way over to her, Benedict slid down beside her, then carefully set his coffee on the other side. "No. I am asking you out because I like your company. I missed you when you were gone." *So much*... He managed to catch those words as he started again, "If it helps the hospital, that would be a bonus. But…" he hesitated "…it feels wrong for me to say I'm glad you're back because I know you left to be with your fiancé. Your ring hand is empty, so I assume that is not a happy story."

He might not like the darkness, but it did make it easier to speak the truth.

"It's not," Penny confirmed, and her head knocked against the elevator. "It's not a happy story at all. You still haven't answered my question. Why is faking a relationship to help public relations for the new maternity unit so important to you? I understand your sister-in-law lost her baby, but given enough time, the funds will come in. The hospital is hosting multiple events over the next few months."

"That won't raise all the money necessary." Benedict's tone was harsher than he'd intended. "And until that unit is in place, we will have mothers who don't make it here to be with their babies before…" The words trailed off, and Penny's hand lay over his before giving it a gentle squeeze.

"There was one last week, and there will be another. It's already heartbreaking. I know we get more NICU graduates than losses. But that doesn't change the fact that if we can have a ward with high-risk patients, it will help them and their babies. Studies have shown how important skin-to-skin contact is, how infants recognize the sound of their mother's voice before they are born. If we can give them the best chance..." He choked up. "I will do anything to make that happen."

And he would. He'd seen the devastation in Amber's life. She'd spent weeks in bed, cried until she couldn't cry anymore and second-guessed everything she'd done, looking for a reason why she'd gone into labor early. He hadn't had the words or knowledge to be much help. But he had that knowledge now. He could help others, do his best to prevent pain.

"And I promise I won't do anything to hurt you," Benedict offered. He didn't know why the promise fell from his lips, but it felt right in the darkened elevator.

A sigh echoed from Penny as she shifted beside him. "That's a sizable promise."

"And one I intend to keep. Promise. I promised myself when we lost little Olivia that I'd do my best to ensure others weren't in the same position. The goal is so close now...waiting...it..."

He choked as the memories invaded his brain. He'd fought with his brother, not knowing he would never get a chance to make it up, then he hadn't been able to protect the woman Isiah loved and the child they'd made. He couldn't change those things, but he could do his best to make sure that history didn't repeat itself for others.

"All right." Penny laid her head against his shoulder, then immediately lifted it back up before squeezing his hand again.

All right...was a simple statement with so much meaning. And for just an instant when her head connected with his shoulder, the world had seemed a bit lighter. He understood why she'd yanked it back. But perhaps the dark didn't just affect him.

No, Benedict was not going to go down that slippery path.

"I'll play along for a while. At least through the fundraising carnival. But I have some ground rules."

"No falling in love. Isn't that what they always say in rom-coms?" Benedict chuckled, though the words felt wrong on his lips. It would be so easy to fall in love with Penny. So easy...

"Of course. But I suspect that won't be a problem for us."

Those words tore through him, and he was again grateful for the darkness so she couldn't see how much the assumption hurt. He should be rejoicing that Penny didn't want to form a more permanent connection. That was what he always said on his dates, and if the woman was interested in long-term, he ended things quickly, before emotions became too deep.

If no one got attached, no one would get hurt. It was lonely, but he'd watched his mother's and father's marriages. Watched how two people could claim to love someone, vow in sickness and health, and then toss it away when things got tough.

"Okay," Benedict chimed in, wishing his voice sounded steadier. "What are the ground rules?"

"No deep conversations. No personal questions. No talk of the past—which shouldn't be hard for you, Mr. Closed Book." Penny sighed. "Whatever we do should be light and fun, and if a few posts make it to the hospital's social media, with a plug for the new maternity ward, then great. If not…"

He felt her shoulder rub his as she shrugged beside him.

"It will make it to social media. One of the videos taken of us on the subway was by the public relations director's grandson. She's already got a whole story outlined—assuming we're dating. It's why I wanted to talk to you before she got to you."

"It all makes sense now." Her shoulder bumped his and she laughed. Though the sound wasn't quite as melodic as he remembered.

They were trapped in an elevator, plotting a fake relationship. Of course it wasn't a true laugh.

Still, Benedict mentally made a note to make Penny laugh, really laugh, as soon as he could. After they got out of the dark.

"I hadn't anticipated this though. I wonder if there'll be someone there with a camera when those doors open."

As if on cue, the door shuddered as it was pried open. A bit of light broke through the sliver. Benedict squinted as it hit his retinas, but he also hated the intrusion. "I really am looking forward to spending time with you."

Penny stood and held out her hand. Benedict grabbed it as he stood. He expected her to drop it. Instead, she laid her head against his shoulder and squeezed it tightly. "May as well look real if there are pictures." She took a deep breath before adding, "Here we go."

"Here we go," Benedict confirmed.

CHAPTER THREE

"IF YOUR FROWN gets any deeper, Alice, your face might freeze like that." Penny wagged a finger like their mother before she reached for her earrings.

"I didn't believe that hogwash when Mom used to tell it to us, and I have a master's in nursing and am a neonatal nurse practitioner—just like you. Which means I know the muscles of my face are not going to freeze as I *glare* at you. What are you doing?" Alice picked up Sooty and gave him a quick pat before putting him on the bed.

"Going to a trivia night," Penny turned and smiled at her sister. Mostly to annoy her, but she was actually excited. She and Benedict were going on a date. Sort of... Did it count if you knew it was only pretend?

He'd invited her to the trivia night at his local pub. The fact that he'd remembered her love of trivia had excited her...perhaps a tad too much.

Penny loved finding obscure pieces of knowledge. She'd dreamed of being a contestant on the game show *Ask This* and cried when it was canceled shortly after she was finally old enough to compete. The fact that Benedict was taking her to a new trivia hub was exciting.

That was the main reason she was practically bouncing.

Not because Benedict would be here in less than twenty minutes. This was just a date so she didn't feel bad at telling Susan Jenkins, the hospital's public relations director, that she could use their dating life as hospital publicity fodder.

It wasn't because of the hot man she was expecting at her door. They'd been such good friends so long ago. She hated that she hadn't sought that connection out when she returned. But that friendship represented the old Penny, and she wasn't really that woman anymore.

Was she?

She swallowed as she looked at herself in the mirror. Was that why she'd held herself back from resuming her friendship with Benedict... or was it because the butterflies had returned to her stomach the moment she'd seen him again? Maybe she should change...

Nope. Tonight she was going to have fun, and look adorable while doing it.

"You don't normally wear earrings to trivia

night." Alice crossed her legs as she sat on the bed. "Or that blue dress."

Penny shook her head as she kissed her sister's cheek. "Relax. This is just a date. Or rather a pretend date. Or, well, the point is, you told me to get back out there. Remember showing me the pictures on your phone?"

"I meant you should swipe right and grab a coffee with a cutie! *Not* enter some fake relationship nonsense with Dr. Denbar. I don't want you to get hurt..." Alice wavered, then grabbed her sister's hands "...again."

"I appreciate the concern." Penny meant the words. She really did appreciate it. But the truth was that Benedict and this arrangement were perfect. She could test the dating waters again, without the fear of getting hurt. Like riding a training bike to see if she was ready to step out in the wide scary world again to find her happily-ever-after.

Cuddling with an angry cat for the rest of her days didn't hold much appeal. And she and Benedict had had fun together all those years ago. She'd had so little fun in the last year.

And maybe she would get the butterflies dancing around her stomach to disappear if she spent a little time with him.

She deserved to go out with a hot man, kick butt at trivia and just let the evening happen.

Besides, he'd promised he wouldn't hurt her—not that they would get close, but she wanted to believe it. At least a little. Her intuition swore Benedict meant his words…once she'd have believed it. But this particular "trusty" sense had led to the doors of tragedy once already.

The doorbell rang, and Penny grabbed Alice's wrist as she hopped off her bed. "Stay here."

Alice stuck out her tongue but stayed in place as Penny moved toward the door, trying to ignore the dash of hope in the back of her brain. This was just a nice evening, a fun night with Benedict.

It was fake. But that didn't make her less excited to open the door. That was something she should examine after tonight, or maybe it would be better not to. Safer to ignore.

Her knees nearly collapsed as she stared at the fine man before her. His jeans were tight in all the right places and the light blue sweater he wore highlighted his dark eyes. Her mouth watered at the sight of him before they landed on the flowers in his hands.

"Daisies?"

Benedict smiled as he handed her the small bouquet. "I saw these and thought—" he pushed his hands into his pockets "—you said they were your favorite. Or at least they were all those years ago… I… I just saw them and…"

He repeated the last line and she leaned over and kissed his cheek. "They are still my favorite. Thank you." He'd remembered. She swallowed, trying to force the tiny lump in her throat down as she turned to get a vase.

Mitchel had always said that flowers were a waste. That it was like throwing money down a drain. But Penny loved having fresh flowers on the table. In Ohio, she'd had a small green space where she'd grown a few veggies in pots. She'd mentioned that she wanted some flowers for her birthday and Mitchel had surprised her with rosebushes.

They'd been pretty but when Penny said she didn't know anything about growing roses, Mitchel had snapped and said they were her favorite flower so she should know. She'd reminded him that her favorite flowers were daisies, and he'd blanched. Then recovered by making her believe that she must have said it once. And she'd agreed... That still stung.

That Benedict could remember an offhanded comment all those years ago touched her heart. And the walls she'd built around it shuddered.

Just a bit.

Mentally shaking herself, Penny put the flowers in water. It was a nice gesture. Sweet, even. But that didn't change the fact that this evening was pretend. She needed to remember that.

"Are you ready for trivia night?" Benedict asked as she followed him through the front door.

"Absolutely!" Penny beamed. Tonight was going to be lighthearted and fun. Just what she needed.

"Who discovered penicillin?"

Benedict popped his hand over the buzzer before Penny got to it, only the second time this evening he'd beaten her to the buzzer and proudly announced, "Who is Alexander Fleming?"

"Yes," the announcer stated as he dropped another point on the board for the Donut Call List team.

"You don't have to answer in the form of a question, Benedict." Penny's foot brushed his calf and his blood heated at the simple touch. Her cheeks were tinged with pink and a touch of salt from her margarita was on the side of her lip.

He reached up and brushed the small crystal away doing his best to ignore the growing bead of desire for the woman across from him. She'd answered nearly every question. They'd only lost points when one of the other teams managed to hit their buzzer before she did.

But she wasn't arrogant or showing off what was a truly impressive body of knowledge on things from the space race to reality television stars. The other teams had grumbled when she took the first three rounds, but those grumbles had turned into looks of awe as she just kept the answers coming.

"I got excited. I knew that one and hit the buzzer first!" Benedict could feel the brilliant smile on his lips. When was the last time he'd had so much fun?

"All right, lightning round time. Not that there is much of a competition." The announcer gestured to the board and the room let out a soft laugh, though there were a few grumbles mixed in.

"Ooh. I love lightning rounds." Penny rubbed her hands together. Her eyes sparkled as her fingers hovered near the buzzer.

She was gorgeous. And it wasn't just the blue dress that hugged her curves in all the right places, or the blue eyes that seemed to call to him. When he was with her, his body seemed to relax. Tension he never realized he was holding evaporated when she kissed his cheek after he handed her the daisies. *Daisies.*

He'd forgotten that detail, though his brain had clearly filed it away somewhere. When walking past the flower shop on the corner by their townhome, he'd seen the flowers in the window and the memory had switched on.

Penny laughing and saying that daisies were the happiest flowers. That they symbolized purity and innocence in the language of flowers. He hadn't even known that flowers had meanings until he'd met her. But her talking about how she loved their bright yellow centers and white petals had made him smile and so he'd showed up with the bouquet.

To a fake date.

Except it doesn't feel pretend.

That was such a dangerous thought. Such a dangerous longing. He'd promised her nothing deep. No talk of the past. Normally that would suit him perfectly. No chance of getting hurt or hurting others. But he wanted to know Penny.

Wanted to know everything about her. Wanted to wipe away the look of pain he sometimes saw cross her eyes, wanted to see the smiles she'd delivered so easily before return. He just wanted her.

"Are you ready?" Penny tapped his thigh with her hand that wasn't by the buzzer and electricity shot down Benedict's leg.

Maybe he should have told Susan that they were just two colleagues who lived close enough together that they rode the same subway car to work.

That would have been the safer option. But he'd do anything to help raise the funds for the new maternity ward. He'd promised his tiny niece he'd do all he could. At that time, his word was all he had. He would not disappoint her memory.

"Are you going to let me answer any of the questions?" Benedict tapped her hand by the buzzer. The urge to pull her hand into his, to hold it, hold her was nearly overwhelming. But he wouldn't interrupt the lightning round. She deserved to be crowned champion tonight.

"If you hit the buzzer before me." She grinned and the dimple appeared again. A happy Penny was the prettiest thing he'd ever seen.

He laughed and gestured to the button, making a dramatic show of taking second place to her expertise. Though they were technically a team.

"The www stands for this in a website."

Penny hit the buzzer. "World wide web."

"I knew that one." Benedict winked and Penny grinned. This was the best date he'd ever been on.

"Who named the Pacific Ocean?"

"Lots of people." Benedict laughed as Penny playfully glared at him and hit the buzzer.

"Ferdinand Magellan." She nodded as the announcer placed another mark on the board.

"I stand by my answer." Benedict let his finger hover by hers. "Lots of names were probably used for the Pacific. It's just his we know."

"Last question."

"We got this." Penny lifted her shoulders as she looked at him.

"You do." Benedict confirmed as he looked to the announcer.

"In the language of flowers, what is the meaning of a daisy?"

Penny dinged in but before she could answer, Benedict piped up, "Innocence and purity. According to Celtic legend, whenever a child died, God sprinkled the flowers over the earth to cheer up parents. They are sometimes given to mothers, since Nordic mythology says they were Freya's favorite flower."

"We'll accept innocence and purity," the announcer stated as he marked the final points on the board. "Surprising absolutely no one, Donut Call List is the winner tonight. See you all next Tuesday. And maybe study up. Looks like there is a new champ in town."

Benedict clapped with the rest of the room and turned his gaze to Penny. She was sitting nearly still as she stared at him. "Do you know the meanings of many flowers?"

"Only daisies." Benedict shrugged. "I used to get coffee at the hospital coffee bar with a woman who loved them." He winked. "She spent the better part of one shift telling me all about them. There's a Roman myth too, but he interrupted me before I could explain."

Her bottom lip shook as she reached for his hand. "You remembered my whole speech about a flower?"

"It was important to you." Benedict stroked her fingers, loving the simple touch. That felt like so much more.

"Hey, any chance you want to join our team next week?"

Penny blinked as she turned to the man standing next to them. "Join your team?"

"Sure." He smiled and ignored Benedict. "We'd love to have you join us. It would be nice to have a pretty girl to look at while we..." He coughed and pulled at the back of his neck. "Besides, you wiped the floor with everyone tonight, and you were basically a table of one, doll." He leaned over her, his eyes traveling toward her breasts before he ratcheted them back up.

"My boyfriend answered the last question. And did so brilliantly. He was just letting me show off." Penny pulled her hand from Benedict's as she crossed her arms over her chest. "Thanks for the offer but no thanks. Have a nice night."

The man stumbled just a bit and put his hand on the table. "Oh, come on. Don't be like that, cutie. I mean you're smart, sure, but..."

He saw Penny clench her teeth and Benedict

stood. "I think Penny eloquently told you no. Go back to your table."

The guy shook his head and threw a look at Penny. "Don't get too attached to this one. I've seen him with a different broad in here every few weeks. Not sure you're the only one using the title *boyfriend* with him."

Benedict felt his mouth fall open as the guy sauntered back to his table. He didn't know what to say. They weren't even really boyfriend and girlfriend. He wasn't sure if Penny had used that term to keep the jerk away or because she was trying to test it in preparation for its use over the next few weeks at the hospital.

He dated regularly. And he brought many of those dates here. It was a quaint local pub that was within walking distance of the National Mall if they wanted to take a stroll in the evening. But hearing it thrown at Penny, used as a weapon, sent a sick feeling through him.

"Are you okay?" Penny's voice was a quiet salve to the unexpected turmoil pulsing through him.

"I feel like I should be asking you that?" Benedict offered a smile that he hoped didn't feel too fake. There were too many emotions tipping through him. Ones that part of him desperately wanted to avoid.

"Not my first time dealing with a jerk at a

bar." Penny sighed as she looked up at the board. "When I first started going to trivia nights, I intentionally waited to answer questions, or spaced the right answers out to avoid making other teams—of men—uncomfortable. But Alice told me if they couldn't handle a chick beating the pants off them, that was their problem."

A little of the weight lifted off his shoulders. "Your sister does have a way with words."

Penny laughed, a real laugh, and his heart lifted even further. "She does. And in this case, she was right. Never make yourself sound less intelligent to make others feel more comfortable."

"An excellent plan." Benedict reached for her hand and was glad when she didn't pull it away. "Want to get out of here and go for a walk?"

"Yes." Penny beamed as he gestured for the check. "It's a really nice night."

He nodded. It was a nice night. But the truth was that he wasn't ready to say good night. He'd spend as much time with Penny as she'd allow. Another feeling that should worry him, but with her by his side, worries refused to materialize.

The cool night air wrapped around her, and Penny wished she'd brought a light jacket. Washington, DC, in late March seemed to hover between unseasonably warm days followed by frost warnings. She hadn't considered that when she'd chosen the blue dress, which she knew high-lighted her curves and eyes. It was a silly choice for a pretend date, but it had been over a year since she'd been out with someone, and she'd wanted to look cute.

No. She'd wanted to look sexy. Desirable.

"You're cold." Benedict shook his head while he looked around the illuminated National Mall, then lifted his sweater off and handed it to her.

Penny opened her mouth to protest, though her tongue paused as she caught a glimpse of the abs under Benedict's undershirt before he pulled it down. He was gorgeous!

"I insist," Benedict stated before she could force the protest from her lips. "I'm hot-blooded. The chill doesn't bother me. And I am not quite ready to call it a night."

Penny slid the sweater over her shoulders and shivered, warmed by Benedict's heat. His scent wafted over her as Penny hooked her arm through his. Her heart hammered instructions for her to lean her head on his shoulder. But she ignored the impulse. She was already crossing so many lines that she'd mentally set for herself to avoid getting too close to him.

Walking arm and arm was already pushing the boundaries. But the night was too perfect for her to care. Besides, she was using these few weeks as an opportunity to dip her toe back in the dating water. May as well take full advantage.

"I'm not ready to head home either. Tonight was fun. Thanks for taking me to trivia. My schedule is too irregular to join an actual team, and it's not as much fun on your own. Alice prefers dance clubs to trivia night. I think I cramp her style a little with my homebody tendencies. Not that she would complain—well, she would, but not too loudly.

"On this topic," Penny added before chuckling.

"It's nice the two of you are so close," Benedict murmured, and she heard the undertone of pain there.

"Bit of a requirement for military brats. We were the only friend we got to keep. I've always been a little jealous of people that grew up in the same room their whole lives." She pulled her hand away from his. She was enjoying the connection a little too much. "Are you and your brother close?"

It was the wrong question. Penny knew it the instant it left her lips, but there was no way to draw it back in.

"We were," he replied softly. "He died when I was nineteen."

"Oh, Benedict, I'm so sorry." Penny's heart ached for him, but he seemed to barely register her response. He was lost in his memories. Before he could pull too far away from her, Penny grabbed his hands and pulled him toward the reflecting pool.

"Did you know that in 1939 Marian Anderson was prevented from singing at Constitution Hall because of her race? So, Eleanor Roosevelt petitioned her husband to let her sing here. Seventy-five thousand people are said to have listened to her concert here on Easter Sunday."

"Distracting me with interesting facts?" Benedict sighed and dropped one of her hands, but he linked fingers with her other.

It was such a tiny motion, but the feel of his hand in hers touched the lonely part of her soul, banishing it. At least for a little while.

"Maybe. We promised each other nothing serious over the next few weeks. And I know that your privacy is important to you."

Benedict's free hand traced along her cheek, and she shivered. Though it had nothing to do with the evening chill. "You notice everything, don't you?"

"One of the things that makes me a good nurse, I suppose." Penny's eyes traced the outline of his lips. Did he start his kisses softly, pulling you in until the world melted away? Or in a rush that left you breathless?

"Maybe," Benedict's voice mused as his eyes

seemed to drink her in. "But I think it's because you see the truth in people."

She felt her lips dip down. There was a time when she might have boasted that reading people was a skill of hers. That she noticed things no one else did. Then she'd gotten engaged to a married man. Couldn't say you read people well after such a colossal failure.

"Don't say it isn't true." His soft words echoed through her.

She dipped her head, pulling away from his soft touch, though she didn't drop his hand. "I'm not the only one who watches people." That was a safer response, one that kept the talk far away from Mitchel.

"Guess not." Benedict sighed. "Thank you. Not sure I ever said that by the way. I really do appreciate you agreeing to pretend for me."

"Right." *Pretend.* The word caught in her heart. This evening was lovely, but it wasn't anything more. Which was good because she wasn't looking for more from it. This was supposed to be lighthearted, fun. A trial. Nothing serious.

If only she could wall away the romantic nature of her heart.

"It is important. Though I admit that I am using you a bit." Penny shrugged as she pulled her hand from his.

"Using me?" Benedict raised an eyebrow as she stared at him.

"Yep." She tried mimicking the sassy sound she'd heard Alice use when she video-chatted with men from her dating apps. How had she gotten so out of practice with flirting? Not that she'd ever really been a top-notch flirter. But she hadn't been this bad. Maybe it was a good thing she was practicing with Benedict.

"I haven't been on a date since I ended things with my fiancé. These next few weeks are me slowly easing my way into it. Little rusty in the flirtation department. As you can probably tell."

"No, I can't tell. But then I've thought you were smart, adorable and downright gorgeous since about five minutes after I met you."

His smile sent thrills chasing through her. "That is an excellent line, Benedict."

"Not a line." He stepped a little closer. "You are adorable, gorgeous and one of the most intelligent people I have ever had the benefit of knowing."

"If this was a romantic comedy, this is the part of the movie where I jump into your arms and kiss you." Penny raised a brow and leaned a little closer, waiting to see if he'd pull back. When he didn't, Penny decided to let her inhibitions down. What good was pretend-dating Dr.

Benedict Denbar if she didn't at least get to see how the man kissed?

"Kiss me." The soft demand left her lips, and if she'd been uncertain, the slow smile spreading across Benedict's lips would have cemented the need in her belly. God, the man was hot.

His lips were soft as they grazed hers. He pulled her closer, the heat of his body echoing through her. She moved without thinking as she wrapped her hands around the nape of his neck. The world slowed as she relished the feel of his body next to hers.

When he deepened the kiss, her soul exploded. If she was ever given the option to pause time, this was the moment she'd choose to run on a loop.

"Penny."

Her name on his lips reached through her senses as she pulled back. "Wow."

"Wow, indeed," Benedict echoed. "We should probably get you home."

That was the safe answer. The responsible answer. But Penny had spent her life choosing the safe path, looking for the responsible choice. And she was alone. For one night, she wanted to live in the moment. Choose excitement without thinking too much.

"Or you could come home with me." Penny ran her hand along his chin, enjoying the bit of stubble under her fingers. Would it feel as good on her skin if he kissed her again? She hoped so.

"Penny." Benedict dipped his lips to hers, barely connecting before pulling back. "Nothing would make me happier. But…"

She laid her finger over his lips before he could say anything. "We're two single adults, who enjoy each other's company. It doesn't have to change anything."

Benedict kissed her again, not as deeply as before but with a fire that clung to her. He wanted her. Just as she wanted him. It felt amazing, and she wanted to chase the feeling, at least for tonight.

"Alice is probably in her room," Penny whispered as she unlocked her door. "Sleeping," she added, though she doubted her sister was actually asleep. But she did not want her bouncing out to ask about tonight. At least not yet.

"Sleeping?"

Benedict's question hit her back. She heard the doubt, but he didn't press.

She silently closed the door and motioned for him to follow her. The thirty steps to her room never seemed so long. But then she'd never walked them before desperate to kiss the man inches behind her.

Flicking on the light, she closed her bedroom

door and turned. Then she carefully lifted his sweater off. "I don't need this anymore." She dropped it on the chair by the small desk.

"No, you don't." Benedict stepped closer and ran his fingers down her arms. "You are so beautiful."

"So are you." Penny smiled as she let her fingers wander to the edge of his shirt before dipping underneath it. His skin was warm, and fire licked up her arm as she ran her hand along his skin.

His head dipped and this time the kiss wasn't soft. The demand of his lips sent pulses of need rippling through her as she let her fingers trace along his stomach grazing the band of his pants before rising.

His hands gripped hers, their fingers tangling together. "If you keep touching me like that, I fear tonight will be over far too fast. And I plan to savor every minute."

"Savor?" Penny whispered as she dropped her lips along the edge of his chin, enjoying the shudder that rippled through him.

"Absolutely," Benedict murmured before he sent his lips to the base of her neck, slowly kissing his way down her collarbone, pulling her dress off one shoulder as his lips caressed her.

She reached for the zipper on the side of her dress, slid it down before pushing the dress to the floor. Cool air hit her skin, and Penny froze. She was really here, with Benedict. Need cascaded through her as the reality stormed across her brain.

"Penny?" Benedict's kisses paused as he put both his large dark hands on the sides of her face, cradling her so carefully. "This stops now, if that's what you want."

She smiled and shook her head. "I want you." She meant the words. She wanted him. *All of him.*

Letting his fingers drip along the top of her breast, Benedict followed the motion with his lips. As her bra fell away, need clawed through her. His touch was too much and not enough at the same time.

The back of her knees hit the bed, and Benedict cradled her as she carefully lay back. Then he dropped his lips to her skin once more. His fingers slid down her thigh, inching ever closer to her core, but never touching her where she needed him.

"Benedict." His name felt like a mantra as it echoed in the room. "Benedict." His lips trailed along the top of her panty line and her breath hitched as he slid her panties to the floor. "Benedict."

"Penny."

Her back arched as his lips traced their way up

her thighs. *Dear God.* When his tongue traced the bud at the top of her mound, Penny nearly screamed. Benedict's fingers matched the slow motion of his tongue along her thigh before he pressed a finger inside her. Her body erupted and the night broke around her.

"Benedict." Penny sat up and drew him close, kissing him deeply as she pulled his undershirt off and dropped it to the floor. "It's hardly fair that you've seen me naked, and I've yet to gaze on you."

She loved the smile tracing on his lips before he bent to kiss her. "Then I should oblige."

"You should," Penny chuckled as she undid the button of his pants and slid them and his boxers to the floor as one. Her breath caught as she stared at him. He was magnificent.

She let her fingers trace along the edge of his manhood, enjoying the looks of desire flickering across his eyes. His hands cupped her face again as she stroked him. "I want you." She met his gaze as she reached for the condoms in her top drawer.

"I need you," Benedict whispered as she carefully slid the condom down his length. "Penny." He kissed her and pulled her up before sitting on the bed and pulling her to his lap.

Her breath hitched as she slid down his length and wrapped her legs around his waist. One hand cradled her carefully as she began to move, enjoying the sensation running through her body almost as much as she enjoyed watching the pleasure float along Benedict's face.

His mouth met hers, their tongues dancing as their bodies melded together. Her rhythm picked up. Need driving her ever closer to the edge. When his thumb reached between their bodies, pressing against her, pleasure shot through her and she lost all sense of everything but the man holding her close.

His hips rose to meet hers, driving need through her. "Penny." He sighed as he crested.

Was there a better sound than her name on his lips?

Leaning her head against his chest, Penny felt so many things as he stroked her back and dropped a light kiss along her head. Finally breaking the connection between them, Penny reached for her robe and draped it around herself.

No words came as she watched Benedict dress. Tonight had been so perfect. But asking him to stay seemed like a step too far. She refused to regret what had happened tonight, but she wasn't going to ask him to stay.

No matter how much her heart cried out for it. It needed to put all its romantic leanings aside and just enjoy the moment.

"I had fun tonight." Penny stepped into his

arms, inhaling his scent. Desperate to draw this out for a few more minutes.

"Me too." Benedict kissed her lips, holding her tightly, like he wasn't quite ready to say goodbye either. "When are you free again?"

Joy shot through her. Maybe it was silly given that they'd promised to see this through until after the first fundraiser, but she wanted to see him again. "Friday." The answer echoed around her.

"Then it's a date." His eyes lit up as he dropped another kiss against her lips.

She laughed and nodded. "Sure." She walked him to the door. "Good night, Benedict."

He bent to kiss her lips and paused just before they touched.

Penny didn't have to turn to know that Alice was watching him.

He dropped a swift kiss on Penny's lips. "Good night, Penny. Alice." Then he was gone.

"That didn't seem super fake." Alice's words were out before Penny got the door closed.

"But it was fun." Alice's frown wavered at Penny's statement. "Very fun."

"I don't want you to get hurt." Alice hugged her tightly.

"I won't. This is just fun. We both agreed. And I desperately need fun. Promise. This doesn't have a fairy-tale ending. I know that; so my heart is in no danger." It hammered in her chest, but she ignored it. This was just fun… It was.

Alice pursed her lips, a bit of disbelief hovering in her eyes. But she didn't say anything.

CHAPTER FOUR

"I saw you're scheduled to work the go-fish booth at the carnival." Dr. Cooke sighed as he handed over the tablet chart. "I got stuck with the ring toss."

"That should be fun," Benedict offered as he looked over the notes from the previous shift.

"Sure." Dr. Cooke rolled his eyes. "Except, carnivals, fundraising dinners and rubbing elbows with donors were not the main reason I went to med school. But since I don't have a cute nurse to hang on my arm on social media posts, I'm starting at a disadvantage in the competition for Dr. Lioness's position."

The insinuation that the only reason he might be at the top of the promotion pool was because of the recent media attention his and Penny's emergency rescue and relationship had generated rubbed Benedict raw. But not as much as the label of *cute nurse* on Penny. She *was* cute.

Adorable. Intelligent. And sexy. So sexy. His

mouth watered at the thought of her, at the memory of the feel of her skin under his fingers.

But she was their colleague and *cute* was the last term Dr. Cooke should be using, particularly with the derision sliding through the man's voice.

A wave of fury rippled through him. As if the nurses on this floor didn't run this unit like a fine machine. As if he or Dr. Cooke could handle any of their duties without the army of women and men RNs ensuring their patients stayed stable.

"Penny Greene is much more than a cute nurse." He barely kept his tone of voice civil, but if Dr. Cooke heard the anger bubbling under the words, he didn't react to it.

"Is Penny going to help you with the booth?" Dr. Cooke raised a brow, and Benedict pushed his emotions aside. It wouldn't do Penny, or him, any good to argue with one of the physicians. Particularly Dr. Cooke. The man's petty streak would have made his mother proud.

"I haven't asked her." Benedict mentally added that to his to-do list. It would make the Wald's Human Resources Department happy, but that wasn't his main incentive. In fact, if he were to make a list, the attention they might draw to the event was near the bottom. He liked spending time with Penny. Time flew with her. The weight of the past that never seemed to leave him lifted when he was with her.

Laughter was easy. Smiles abundant. It might be a temporary arrangement, but Benedict was going to treasure every moment. "But I plan to."

"Will she come with you to the two fundraising dinners too?"

"I hope so." Benedict regretted the words as soon as they were out of his mouth. They were the truth, but Penny had only agreed to fake date through the first fundraiser. Suddenly the ticking clock she'd set echoed in his heart. One night with Penny wasn't enough.

He wanted…

Again, words failed him.

Holding Penny, watching passion coat her skin, had been one of the best moments of his life. If he concentrated, he could almost feel the ghost of her lips on his. He swallowed as need wrapped around his heart. Maybe he could convince her to stick with him through the first fundraising dinner, and by then maybe whatever burned between them would fizzle out.

His brain laughed as his heart scoffed. He wasn't sure any time would be enough with Penny, but he wasn't going to focus on that now.

"Really going to keep one around for two months then?" Dr. Cooke laughed and looked at his watch. "I'll see you tomorrow." Then he was gone.

But Dr. Cooke's words clung to the air around him.

So what if he didn't do long-term connections? All the women he'd been with had been fine with that arrangement.

But was he?

The air seemed to evaporate from the room as the question reverberated around his skull. He was fine with his life.

He was.

So why was his heart pounding?

Benedict tried to shake the feeling from his soul as he opened the tablet to review the status of his current cases.

Last night he and Penny had given in to the desires coating them. They were both single, enjoyed their evening together. There was nothing wrong with the choice. Countless single people did the same on their dates. It didn't have to mean anything.

Except. Need pooled through him. Except Benedict was already contemplating how to extend this escapade for a couple of months. But that didn't mean he wanted a long connection. He just… Well, he didn't have the time or inclination to think it through now.

"You all right?" Charles, one of the counselors who worked on the floor, asked as he leaned over the nurses' station.

"Yeah." Benedict nodded before adding, "I think so."

Charles put his drink down and looked at Benedict. Really looked.

He barely managed to keep from rocking on his heels under the scrutiny.

"I've asked you that question countless times. You've never answered with anything other than, *yeah, I'm fine* or *yep* in the six years I've known you." Charles's brow furrowed as he slid his tablet under his arm. "Want to talk about it?"

Benedict understood that the counselors were there for the patients, their families and the staff. This was a trying field that had more bad days than good sometimes. But he'd never talked to Charles, or to any of the counselors on staff. He'd seen a therapist for a short while following his brother's and niece's passing, but nothing more.

"It's really nothing." Benedict shrugged. "Just a comment from Dr. Cooke about how much I date."

"I suspect he's just jealous. The man would love to be a playboy like you." Charles smiled. "Jealousy has a way of interfering in most things."

"I'm hardly a playboy." Was this really the reputation he had?

Alice strolled to the nurses' station and shot

him a withering glare before dropping her radio in the charging station, grabbing another and heading into the room of Jeremiah Blake.

Charles let out a whistle. "If looks could kill. Did a date with Alice go wrong? Workplace breakups can…"

"No," Benedict interrupted. "I am dating her sister, Penny." The words were out, and Benedict was struck by how uncomfortable they made him. The relationship wasn't a secret…only the temporariness of it.

HR had posted two pictures of them, one in the unit with the note about the fundraiser and another that showed a headline printed out from a news site regarding their rescue after the metro trains detached. But suddenly part of him wished the rest of the world didn't know.

Not because he wanted to hide Penny. No. Because he wanted to keep her. That terrifying thought stunned him. Each post, each acknowledgment was a reminder that it wasn't more than an act.

"Oh," Charles answered. "Well…" His cheeks heated, and he rubbed the back of his neck. "Sisters can be protective, and the Greene sisters are closer than most."

He paused. "If you need to talk about anything, just know my door is open. Or if you'd prefer we set up a talk with someone outside the hospital, that can be arranged too." He handed Benedict his card, bright yellow with bold letters. He'd handed them to parents hundreds of times. A bright color so it could be spotted in full purses and crammed wallets.

Bright and hard to ignore.

But he was fine. Better than fine. He started to put the card on the desk, then slid it into his pocket as he started his rounds.

"There you go." Penny's voice was soft in Indigo Narvar's barely lit room. The little girl had been born at not quite twenty-seven weeks with underdeveloped lungs. She'd battled a round of pneumonia that had seriously concerned the staff. Her progress over the last three weeks had been slow but steady.

"Are you sure I'm not hurting her?" Piper's worried cry echoed as she gently stroked her daughter's back while she lay on her chest. "I don't want to pull any of her tubes."

"You won't," Penny encouraged as she hovered over the mom and her baby. "Kangaroo care is one of our babies' favorite things. And studies have shown it's good for their heart and breathing. I promise she is doing fine. See." Penny pointed to the monitors and tracking devices on the wall that monitored nearly everything Indigo did. "If anything was wrong, one of these alarms would be going off."

"Nurse Greene is right," Benedict reinforced as he slid to the side and looked at Indigo. She'd weighed less than three pounds when she was born, but after almost five weeks, she was starting to look less fragile. Infants grew at a fast pace but watching the NICU patients put on weight and start to look like all the other happy chunky infants always warmed Benedict's heart.

"You are doing great." He pulled up Indigo's chart and looked over it. "She gained half a pound this week and is using less supplemental oxygen."

Piper closed her eyes before gently laying her lips on her daughter's head. "I love you."

"Why don't we give you a few minutes?" Penny smiled and looked at Benedict as she nodded to the door.

"You won't go far?"

"Nope," Penny assured her. "We'll rush in if there are any problems. But you're doing great, Mom." Her breath hitched a little on the last word.

Benedict pursed his lips as he looked at her. He wasn't sure what had happened with her engagement, wasn't sure how it had affected her, but did she still yearn for a family of her own?

She'd be an excellent mother. Loving, kind, but stern when necessary. A deep well of desire floated across his chest. That life couldn't be his, however much he yearned to have Penny to himself, to cherish her, protect her...

He'd vowed to protect his brother, to come to each of his races, to check his car, to ensure it was ready. Isiah had sworn he was done with illegal races after a friend was seriously injured, then he'd abruptly agreed to one more because of the pregnancy. Without telling Benedict the true reason. He'd been furious.

So, he'd stayed home. And broken his promise...

Benedict bit the inside of his cheek, willing the memories away. Rationally he knew that it wasn't anything with the engine that had caused the crash. Knew that his presence there that day wouldn't have accomplished anything. But if they hadn't been at odds, would Benedict have seen the signs after the injury? He would never forgive himself for not taking better care of his brother. As for Penny, whatever kind of family life was in her future, it would never be with him. He couldn't open himself up to that kind of hurt. Love was dangerous.

"You're frowning." Penny tapped his shoulder.

Such a small connection. Yet his body sang. And begged for more.

Trying to keep the moment light, to ignore the increasing bank of emotions Penny raised in him, Benedict nodded to the nurses' station where Alice was looking over notes. "If glaring were an Olympic sport, I think Alice could win gold."

A quiet chuckle escaped Penny's lips, and she waved as Alice looked up at the noise. "When we were growing up, my mother once told Alice that we were working on tact when she said something lost to the memory of time. Alice promptly responded that maybe the rest of us were, but she had all she needed."

She wrapped her arms around herself as her sister headed into another room. "I learned my parents' lessons well and will always resort to tact and diplomacy. But Alice…" She shrugged. "You always know where you stand with Alice. She doesn't hide anything. There are times I wish I was more like her. Though don't tell her that."

Benedict laughed then. "It was the same with Isiah and me. I think we both coveted something the other had. School came easy for me, but he struggled. But he excelled at making connections, street smarts and reading people. I've gotten better at those things, but as a teenager, I craved the easiness with which he started a conversation. I guess sibling rivalry is universal even if you love them more than anything."

Penny's mouth opened, closed, then opened again. "I like hearing about your brother."

The statement sent a wave of panic through him. What had he done? As a general rule, he didn't talk about his brother but Penny had him opening up in a way that was entirely foreign to him.

An alarm echoed from Indigo's room, and Penny spun on her feet. Benedict was directly behind her.

Indigo's oxygen levels had dropped, and tears were streaming down her mother's face. "She moved and I tried to adjust her like you showed me." Panic laced the frantic words, and she stroked her baby's back. "Indigo, Indigo…"

"Let me." Benedict gently lifted the little one and was glad to see that the oxygen tube was kinked. It was a common enough issue, particularly as their patients got more mobile and pulled at the cords attached to them.

Once it was adjusted, the alarm slowed and finally silenced.

Indigo shifted in Benedict's hands and her eyes fluttered open. She locked eyes with her mother and let out a cooing noise. "I think she's ready for Mom now." Benedict started toward Piper, but the woman held up her hands, her eyes still brimming with tears.

"I shouldn't. I didn't even think about the oxygen cord. I was just so happy she was moving around on my chest like her brother used to do. I'm supposed to protect her, and I failed."

"No, you didn't." Benedict shook his head.

He'd watched parents take blame for all sorts of things in the NICU. They worried they were responsible for their child ending up here. Occasionally decisions they made had resulted in a premature birth, but in his experience, that was rare and usually the result of untreated addiction.

But knowing there was nothing you'd done wrong and accepting it were two very different things. As he well knew.

"Your daughter is fine." Penny's kind words carried across the room as she wrapped her arms around Piper. "Even if you had made a mistake, which you didn't, everything is okay."

Piper sniffled. "It wasn't so hard with Larkin. He was born right at forty weeks." She hiccupped, "But I was also in my twenties, not forty-two."

"That isn't an abnormal age to have a baby," Benedict coaxed as he handed Indigo back to her mother. He knew that she and her husband had been shocked by her pregnancy. After years of trying, following their son's birth, they'd given up and had been looking forward to the next phase of life when they'd found out about the pregnancy.

She kissed Indigo's forehead as she carefully cradled her daughter. "Every time I am here, and when I'm at home, in her empty nursery, I keep thinking what-if."

"You can't play that game." Penny offered Piper a smile. "What-ifs get you nowhere."

Penny was right. But Benedict also knew that those words were easily spoken. The action behind them… Well, some people never managed to stop wondering what-if. His throat closed as he pushed his own what-if questions away.

Before he could say anything else, Penny continued, "I know those are easy words for me to say. And I have my own life situations where I still wonder what I could have done better, or different. But all those questions do at night is keep me up. I promise, you did nothing wrong."

Piper bit her lip. "I just worry I'm a bad mom. You know, I wasn't exactly thrilled when I found out I was pregnant." Her shoulders shuddered as a truth Benedict suspected she'd been holding on to for some time slipped into the room.

"Want a little secret all nurses know?" Penny didn't wait for an affirmative answer. "Actual bad parents *do not* worry that they are bad parents."

The tips of Piper's lips rose a bit. Penny had found the perfect words.

"She's right." Benedict nodded. He checked his watch and looked at Penny. "I need to see to another patient. Can you stay with Indigo and Piper for a few more minutes?"

"Of course," Penny answered.

The smile on her face sent another wave of emotions wandering through him. He slipped from the room as Penny helped Indigo and her mother readjust to prepare for breastfeeding. While the NICU substituted formula, when necessary, they encouraged as many mothers as possible to pump breast milk and to try breast-feeding when their babies were medically stable.

As he started for the next patient's room, Penny's words about worries rattled around his brain.

What kept her awake at night? What what-ifs did she replay?

They'd promised that their connection over the next month or so was light, that personal questions were off-limits. It was Penny's rule, but Benedict hadn't minded. But he hated the idea that she lay awake at night wondering what-if. He did the same, far too often.

He knew how sad and lonely that was. It was a state he'd accepted for himself, but the fact that Penny did the same tore through him. She deserved better.

Her feet ached and her body felt heavy as Penny followed her sister down the pavement toward the metro station. The shift had been long and heartbreaking. A micro-preemie who had arrived from Grace Hospital had passed not long after his father had arrived, frantic at leaving his wife but needing to be with their son. The sound of the father's broken sobs was still reverberating around her brain. She needed a shower, a good cry and at least ten hours of uninterrupted sleep.

Two of those things were easy. The third… Penny rolled her shoulders. She'd been honest with Piper. There were questions that kept her up. Everyone had regrets, but on days when her mind was actively trying to avoid thinking of a tragedy at work, it always seemed to wander to Mitchel.

She knew her ex had hidden his life well. But there'd been signs she'd missed. His refusal to talk about the past. The little hints he'd drop about his life before her, or more likely let slip through the cracks by accident, had been nuggets she'd clung to, trying to get to know him better.

But tonight, it wasn't Mitchel her brain wandered to.

Benedict.

They'd sworn this temporary arrangement was light. Fluffy. Unconnected. It was only meant to be a test before she entered the dating game full-time.

But she wanted to know about Isiah.

In so many of Penny's stories, Alice played a starring role. She smiled as her sister grabbed the rail pull in front of her. "I hear you glared at Benedict today."

Alice stuck out her tongue. "Dr. Denbar is exaggerating, I'm sure. I was nothing but professional."

"I've seen your *only professional* behavior before." Penny leaned against the metro bar. Her body was exhausted, and her soul heavy.

The memory of the father on her shift tonight would not leave her. Torn between his wife and his son, the most terrible day of his life had been made so much worse. And as for the mother who had been separated from her son, who would never get the chance to... Penny's eyes filled with tears. It was the perfect example for why the unit for high-risk mothers was so important. And Penny hated that knowledge. She'd seen it in Benedict's eyes too. The knowledge, and the pain it brought.

"Well, I'm worried about you." Alice closed her eyes as she leaned against the pole opposite Penny. "You trust so easily, and always see the best in people. You want the fairy tale and give your heart too freely."

"Not anymore." Penny sighed. "I learned my lesson." She wanted to believe the words. But she wanted to know the man everyone referred to as *a closed book*. She'd gotten a glimpse at the hidden pages of Benedict, and it wasn't enough.

Such a dangerous desire. She'd spent so long chasing the crumbs Mitchel doled out about his past. She'd promised herself she wouldn't do that again.

Still, her heart ached to know about the brother that still meant so much to Benedict.

"Learned your lesson? So much so that you entered a fake relationship with the hospital play-boy so he has a better chance at landing the head of the department job that opens in a month. Sure, sweetie. You keep telling yourself that."

"It's to help with fundraising for the maternity unit."

Alice raised a brow. Penny understood her sister's skepticism. The medical field was full of doctors who went into the position to heal, to make the best of the worst time in people's lives, to help.

But it also had more than its share of social climbers. Men and women who were in the profession for the money and respect it brought. But that wasn't what Benedict was after. She'd never have agreed to the ruse if she thought Benedict was one of those professionals. He truly wanted what was best for his patients. And the high-risk maternity unit was what was best.

"Benedict…"

Butterflies danced across her belly, and she found herself smiling as the man stepped in the metro car just before the doors shut, as if her thoughts of him had conjured him. She was glad he was here. *So glad.*

He tipped his head toward Alice, then moved to stand by Penny. He didn't say anything, but her body felt a little lighter knowing he was so close. It was a silly feeling, especially given the words she'd just spoken to her sister, but Penny didn't care. On days like today, you took whatever comfort you could find.

The metro started up, and she let out a sigh.

"You okay?" Benedict shook his head. "As okay as today allowed anyway."

Penny nodded. She'd spent the first year in the NICU crying herself to sleep after days like today. That didn't happen anymore, but that felt like a loss too. It was important to keep yourself separate from the tragedy.

But what does it mean that I can do that now?

It was a question Penny didn't want to contemplate too closely. At least not today.

"Nothing a hot shower and a mug of tea won't fix." She shrugged, wishing those words weren't the truth. But coping mechanisms were necessary, otherwise she wouldn't be able to help her other patients.

"I usually spend the evening tinkering in my workshop after days like today." Benedict pulled at the back of his neck as the train slowed for the first stop.

"And I go out with friends," Alice added to the conversation before looking from Benedict to Penny. "And I plan to drag my sister with me tonight."

"You do?" Penny felt the words leave her lips before she pursed them and stared at her sister. It was true that on hard days Alice had a few friends that she met up with. They went dancing, and she spun her body around, craving the loud noise, movement and anonymity of the club.

It was not something Penny enjoyed. She always felt out of place, an issue highlighted by the fact that her body did not move to the music the way her sister's did. Alice floated on a dance floor, her body in rhythm to whatever beat played. Penny stomped, against the rhythm, never able to let her body relax despite her sister's coaxing.

"Yes," Alice reiterated. "It will be good for you. Dancing is fun and maybe you'll meet someone." She winked at Penny before turning her attention to her phone.

An uncomfortable silence filled the space between her and Benedict. Their relationship wasn't real. Yes, they were going on dates so she didn't feel like it was truly lying. Yes, they'd spent the night together. They were single and enjoyed each other's company—like countless other singles did.

It didn't matter that, if she closed her eyes, she could still feel his touch on her skin. The memory of his kisses on her body. Her skin heated and she started to lean into him before gripping the bar tighter. She was not going to do that.

"I hope you have fun," Benedict murmured.

Meeting someone shouldn't make her feel like she wasn't being fair to Benedict... So why was her stomach flopping as her cheeks heated?

Penny rolled her eyes before looking down at her shoes. "I'll find a way out of it. I suspect she'll give up when we get to our townhome. She's just..." She let her whispered words die out.

"Protecting you," Benedict filled in the silence. "That's the main role a sibling plays. Or it is supposed to be."

His voice nearly cracked, and she put her hand over his. The connection vibrated between them. She didn't know what he was thinking but she could see the pain radiating behind his eyes. The metro slowed, and she glanced at the stop. Where had the time gone?

"It's our stop." Penny squeezed his hand. "If you ever want to talk..."

"Light and fluffy, remember?" Benedict smiled.

"I know." Penny felt her lips pull to the side, hating the promise she'd dragged from him. But also not wanting to give too much of herself away either. Maybe it wasn't fair to want his secrets when she wasn't willing to give her own. "But the offer still stands."

"Thanks. Enjoy your tea. Or dancing, if Alice holds you to it."

"She won't." Penny patted his hand once more. "She's more bark than bite…though she'd never admit it. Good night, Benedict."

"Night, Penny."

Alice was several feet away when Penny exited the metro car.

"You really want me to go dancing with you?" She moved to her sister's side and matched her quick step.

"No," Alice grumbled. "I mean, you're welcome to, but I know it's not how you process tough days. I just…" She pushed a hand through her hair as she stopped in front of a local restaurant. "I just want you to be happy. If he makes you happy for now—" She held up a hand before Penny could interrupt. "If he makes you happy, then I will keep my thoughts to myself. But your heart is in danger. Whether you want to admit it yet or not."

She huffed out a breath, then tilted her head to the restaurant. "Go on. You'll be much happier with your order of sushi, hot tea and fuzzy slippers than you will be on the dance floor."

Penny kissed her sister's cheek. "I love you, you know that, right?"

"Of course. I'm amazing. And so easy to love." Alice winked, then tilted her head. "I love you. Always and forever, you and me."

"You and me," Penny agreed.

Her sister waved as she turned on the street that would lead her home. Their bond was for life. And Penny had no idea what she'd do without Alice. It would feel like she'd lost a part of herself.

Was that how Benedict felt?

She pulled her phone out and started to type a message to him before putting it back in her pocket.

They'd all had a rough shift. It happened. And everyone had the way they worked through it. For her, it was hot tea, sweatpants and fuzzy slippers. Benedict would be okay. And it wasn't her responsibility to check in on him.

Except it felt like…

No. She was not going to wander down that path. She was going to get her dinner. Have a quick shower and sit in front of the TV with some show she didn't have to follow while she got all her emotions together. Benedict could handle himself.

He could.

Feel like meeting up?

Penny stared at Benedict's text; it was as if her thoughts of him had conjured the words. Her fingers hesitated for only a moment before she typed back.

Want to meet at the National Mall?

Benedict stared at the text from Penny. He'd sent her a message less than an hour after he'd gotten home, asking if she wanted to meet up. He was surprised he'd lasted that long. After all, his fingers had itched from the moment he hit his front door.

The day sucked. There was no other way to describe the loss of little ones. Comforting parents, dealing with the end was never pleasant. Over his decade in the NICU, he'd watched technology advance. Watched the numbers shift in favor of doctors against the fates that would pull souls to them. But it didn't make them gods. Didn't let him snap his fingers and just make everything okay.

When Penny had laid her hand over his, the storm inside him calmed. He wasn't sure what it was about her touch that made his spirit lift, but it was intoxicating. He craved it.

That should make him call a halt to the ruse they were playing. Should make him shut it down.

Tell her they should just be friends…except they were friends. The relationship wasn't real.

There was no need to worry about getting close because it wasn't real. Except it felt… It felt like the beginning of something good. And for the first time in his life, turning away from someone, *from Penny*, didn't seem like an option.

At least not an option he planned to exercise.

His fingers hovered over the screen before he typed.

How about you come here? I have tea.

He held his breath as he pushed Send. As the minutes dragged on with no response, Benedict wished there were a way to recall the message. A way to delete it from the ether. A way to turn back time.

He should have agreed to meet at the National Mall. Or some other neutral space.

I don't have your address.

The words sent an explosion through him. Before he could second-guess the action, he typed out the address and a quick set of directions for how to get to his place from the metro station two blocks away.

See you soon.

He felt the smile pull his lips. A giant grin at odds with the day he'd had. When had that last happened? He smiled, maybe not giant grins, but when had a smile felt like it transported his whole mood?

Benedict didn't want to waste any time on the thought. Instead, he turned on the kettle and grabbed a couple of mugs from the cabinet. All he had was chamomile and English breakfast tea. Not much of a selection to offer a woman who said her coping mechanism was fuzzy slippers and tea.

Glancing at his watch, he shook his head; there wasn't time to run to the grocery on the corner. Even if he did know what to grab, he didn't want to risk missing her arrival. His small stash would simply have to do for now, but he'd make a point to find out if it was better if he stocked something else.

CHAPTER FIVE

THE DOOR TO Benedict's townhome was dark blue. It was the kind of door that screamed for a wreath of colorful flowers to welcome guests, but the door was empty. Not even a welcome mat. None of these thoughts mattered, and for the millionth time since she'd taken the one metro stop from her townhome to his, she wondered what she was doing here.

Her hair was still wet and pulled into a topknot. She had on yoga pants and an athletic top. If she'd had her yoga mat, she'd look just like she did every time she managed to make it to the hot yoga studio.

This wasn't a date. It was… Her mind couldn't find a safe word. It wasn't rational that she was here. She should turn around, go home and make some excuse, but she couldn't force her feet to move.

Her phone buzzed, and her cheeks heated at Benedict's message.

Want me to open the door? Or to pretend I never saw you outside so you can send me a message to say you changed your mind? No pressure either way.

A small giggle escaped her lips before she raised her hand and rapped on the door. She was already here, and already seen. So why not follow through with whatever this was?

The door swung open as soon as she stopped knocking, and she smiled as her body relaxed. "How long have you known I was here?"

Benedict pointed to his doorbell. "It has a camera and sends a notification to my phone. So pretty much the moment you stepped in front of it. But..." he reached for her hand and squeezed it "...you seemed unsure, so..."

"I was wondering if I should have changed, then told myself this wasn't a date, it was just two colleagues meeting up, then told myself that meant I definitely should have changed. I am a champion overthinker!"

"Then you're in good company. I can overthink with the best of them." Benedict started toward the kitchen area of his townhome and pulled up two boxes of tea. "I realized all I had in the townhome was chamomile and English breakfast tea. I contemplated going to the store

on the corner at least fifty times, then worried I
wouldn't be back in time."

Crossing her arms and shaking her head,
Penny let the weight of the worries slide away
from her. Any man who'd worry about a tea selection was a person she'd enjoy spending time
with. "Chamomile is great. A little late for caffeine for me."

"I am not sure my body reacts to it anymore."
Benedict dropped a tea bag into each mug before
picking up the kettle. "Sugar?"

"No." Penny playfully covered her mouth in
horror as Benedict dropped two large spoonsful
of sugar in his own mug. "Alice would appreciate your cup of tea. I swear she prefers tea-fla-
vored sugar water."

Benedict held his mug up to his lips and took
a deep sip before making a face. "Too hot."

Gripping her mug, Penny let the heat seep into
her. She loved tea, and coffee. Pretty much any
hot beverage, but it was this moment she enjoyed
most. The warmth of the drink, waiting for it to
cool, it calmed her. Stabilized her. She'd never
been able to explain the feeling, but it was her
happy place.

"That's boiling water for you." She leaned over
the counter, still holding her mug, and looked at
his lips. So full and close. Swallowing, she pulled
back. "Are you okay?"

"Nothing more than my pride injured."

"That's an injury some people aren't able to take." The words flew from her lips, and she saw the flash of curiosity come over Benedict's features.

Why did I say that?

It was true. Pride destroyed so many things. Mitchel had stayed married because he was worried how it would look to the community to divorce his wife. Not that he'd considered how it would look for the world to discover he was keeping a mistress with a fake engagement ring on her hand in Ohio.

Still, it was his pride that had been injured when his wife and Penny sent him on his way. Not a broken heart. Pathetic.

"Well, my pride has taken many hits over the years, and I've always recovered." Benedict nodded to the couch. "Let's have a seat."

"Many hits?" Penny asked as she sat and crossed her legs on the other side of the couch. It was too much space. Space her heart begged her to close, but she was not going to give in to it. "It's hard to believe you've taken a ton of hits to your pride. Have you seen yourself? You're gorgeous."

Her cheeks heated and she raised her mug to cover her face. *Why the hell did I say that?* Good grief, her tongue had a mind of its own tonight.

At least the statement was true. Benedict was one of the handsomest men she'd ever seen. If he wasn't a physician in the country's top NICU, he could grace the cover of any magazine. It was hard to believe he'd ever felt embarrassed.

"When I was a freshman in high school, the science experiment I'd carefully planned out for advanced chemistry went awry. To this day, I'm not exactly sure what combination of chemicals I mixed wrong. It was supposed to create a rubber-like blue material that expanded and then hardened. I'd done it at home several times perfectly."

He shook his head and raised his mug to his lips. "Instead it made a noxious chemical concoction that forced the school to evacuate, and a hazmat unit was called in. Half the school thought I'd done it on purpose, the other half thought I was a fool. My school record was nearly perfect, so they didn't suspend me, but I spent all summer working at the school to help offset the cost of the cleanup. I was already a gangly nerd. It did not help my reputation."

"Oh, my!" Penny felt her eyes widen. It was hard to imagine the man before her now as an awkward teen but endearing. "That must be quite the story at the high school reunions."

"Maybe."

His gaze shifted and she wondered what he

was seeing. What part of the past he was visiting…and if his brother was there?

The moment passed as he looked at her and raised his mug again. "I don't know. I haven't been home since I left for college."

"Not at all?" That knowledge cut a small wound across her heart. She didn't have a place she considered her childhood home. She'd lived in six different states and three different countries before she'd graduated high school. She'd always been jealous of the people she met who slept in their childhood rooms at holiday and family gatherings. She craved the stability that that life represented for her.

"No." Benedict pursed his lips before adding, "Home isn't exactly a happy place."

His body shifted and before he could pull away, she closed the distance between them and laid her head on his shoulder. Whether he wanted to talk about it or not, she was here.

And painfully aware of how fortunate she was. She might not have a specific house to call a home, but whenever she and Alice and their parents were together, it was a home. A wonderful, joyous home.

She hadn't realized how unique that was until she'd moved away to attend college. How many families were hiding their unhappiness and brokenness behind closed doors and smiling family portraits. "I bet you're a legend there and just don't realize it."

Benedict leaned his head against hers but didn't say anything.

They sat like that for several minutes. Just enjoying not being alone after a long day. No words seemed necessary. Sitting in silent comfort, not needing to fill the quiet was a blessing so few understood.

But in the silence, she let her eyes wander. His townhome was large but sparsely furnished. The white walls were devoid of any pictures, and other than the couch they were sitting on, the coffee table and the television, this room was empty.

It was as if he'd just moved in but hadn't had time to decorate. "How long have you lived here?"

"About six years." Benedict set his mug on the little coffee table in front of him and pulled her into his arms. It wasn't sexual but the intimacy of the moment pulled at her. The two of them, dressed casually, just enjoying the other's company after a long day. It felt so much more intimate than the night they'd spent in each other's arms.

Her heart clenched and she briefly wondered if Alice was right. Surely she wasn't actually in danger of losing her heart here. They were just...

Again, her brain refused to provide a word.

And she didn't want to dwell on it too much. She was happy and content in his arms. That was enough for today.

"My home growing up never had any decoration." His words were quiet but he kept going. "The walls were the same lemon yellow they were when my parents moved in, though by the time I left they looked more sallow than bright. I guess. So I've never really thought too much about decorating. But it does look a little sad, huh?"

"Not sad," Penny stated, though that wasn't entirely true, but she didn't want to hurt his feelings. Didn't want to push away the small intimate piece of him she was seeing. "If you didn't see decorations growing up, why would you necessarily think of them?"

A slow smile spread across his face. It made her belly twist with an emotion she didn't want to name as she kissed his cheek. The platonic kiss felt so unsatisfying. "Besides, it's an easy enough fix." Penny brightened as she looked around. "We moved every few years with my parents' jobs, but in every rented place, my dad made sure we were allowed to paint."

She smiled as the memories floated through her. "Whenever possible, we'd arrive a few days before the army movers. Mom and Dad let Alice and I pick the colors for our room, and once we were older, it was our job to help turn the rented space into our home. I can still remember the bright pink Alice and I chose for our room when we lived in North Carolina. Our room faced the west with this giant window. It was so bright my parents had to invest in blackout curtains so that we would go to bed."

She giggled. "We could be real pains about bedtime."

"I suspect most kids are that way. Siblings that team up are probably able to leverage more command than those that fight all the time."

"Did you and Isiah fight all the time?"

Benedict's gaze shifted again, and he shook his head. "No, but when we did…" He pursed his lips and looked at her. "What colors would you paint if you lived here?"

Penny patted his hand, aware that she'd touched a painful part of his past. Unintentional or not, it still upset her to cause him pain. And a tiny twist of doubt pushed through her at the knowledge that once again he'd started to open up but then pulled back.

But that was fine, because this was just a light and fluffy fake relationship. Except when she was in his arms…

Her body ached as her soul yearned for more. But she was not going to give in to those feelings.

Instead she swiveled in his lap, desperately

aware of the feelings rocking through her as she stared at his kitchen. It was a small open area that led to the living room. He could paint it an accent color and then keep this room neutral with a picture or some plants. If he decided to take this from a hypothetical "change of conversation" topic to the real world. "What's your favorite color, Benedict?"

"Blue."

"Blue." She smiled and gestured with her hand for him to expand. "What kind of blue?"

"Kind of blue?" His dark eyes held hers, and she could see the hint of a smile in the corner of his lips. "Just blue."

Setting her mug down, she playfully hit his shoulder. "There is a whole spectrum of blue. I have a set of pencils that is just shades of blue. Do you mean navy or baby blue? Teal or aqua? The options are endless."

Benedict laughed and wrapped his arms around her, his fingers stroking her back. Did he ache to kiss her as much as she ached to raise her lips to his?

"I have never given blue much thought." He kissed the tip of her nose. "If pressed, I suppose I'd say lighter than navy but darker than baby blue."

"So somewhere around azure or aero would be my guess." Alice kissed his cheek.

"Sure. Aero sounds right." Benedict nodded, playing along, though she knew he didn't actually have any idea what she meant.

"Maybe I should bring my pencils next time. I could show you…" Her mouth dried as she looked at him. "I mean, if you wanted me to come over again." It seemed like such a stupid statement when she was sitting on his lap and discussing paint colors. How quickly she'd lapsed into the idea of this being something more.

"I think I'd really enjoy that." His eyes sparkled with desire.

Before she could overthink it too much, Benedict's lips met hers. The soft brush of them turned demanding as she ran her fingers along the base of his jaw, enjoying the stubble there.

"Penny."

Her name on his lips just after kissing her might be the sweetest sound in the universe. Again, her brain sent a warning shot, but it was easy to ignore when she was in his arms. *Too easy.*

God, Penny. Benedict's mind screamed as his fingers stroked her back. Painfully aware of the thin shirt separating her soft skin from his fingers. He ached for her.

It wasn't where he'd planned this evening to go. When he'd offered her tea, Benedict had truly planned to share a mug and an hour or so of conversation with someone who made it possible for him to forget that the world could be a cruel place. Just some time with a woman who made the hole inside him almost disappear. But as her lips met his again, his body cried out with need.

Her tongue traced his lower lip, and his fingers roamed the top of her waistband.

"Benedict." The softness of his name on her full lips was the most intoxicating thing he'd ever heard.

"Penny." His fingers ran along her chin, enjoying the subtle changes in her blue eyes as they watched him. That color, whatever it was called. Blue with hints of smokiness in the center and a trace of green was his favorite shade of blue. He didn't know if it had a name, but in his mind, it would always be known as Penelope Perfection.

"I want you." Her lips tipped up as her fingers caressed his chest.

"I want you too." *In so many different ways.* He managed to catch those words before he let them loose. He wanted Penny. But not in just "a few moments of pleasure" way.

That wasn't what they'd promised each other though. He knew she hadn't dated much, maybe at all, since whatever happened with her ex-fiancé. She was using this relationship as a trial before reentering the dating world. A way to get all her nervousness out. He was the rebound with no strings attached.

It was what he'd always wanted. But staring into her eyes, with her in his lap, it didn't seem like nearly enough. This might not be a forever situation, but at least he could relish every minute.

Making sure his grip was secure, Benedict stood, ensuring she stayed in his arms. Her lips traveling across his neck made it difficult to concentrate on keeping his feet steady on the stairs, but he managed to make it to his bedroom. Thrills drifted around his body as he set her on his bed.

"Now I really wish I'd done more than throw my hair in a wet topknot and put on yoga pants." Penny's quiet words rocked the room as she sat on her knees and lifted his shirt over his head.

Before she could do anymore, Benedict caught her hands in one of his and let his other linger on the top of the scoop-neck athletic shirt she had on. "You are gorgeous, Penny. So gorgeous." He swallowed as need raced through him. The urge to rip her clothes off and bury himself deep within her, show her how much she called to him was overwhelming, but he was going to enjoy every moment of Penny in his bed.

"Whether you have a messy topknot, which is adorable by the way." He kissed her, enjoying the sigh caught in the back of her throat as he let his free hand roam her delicious backside. "Or the fanciest hair, ever."

Letting go of her hands, Benedict lifted her shirt, and felt his breath hitch at the sight of rosy desire coating her skin. "Whether you are in an athletic top or the blue dress that made my mouth water, you are stunningly beautiful. And I am weak with need just being in the same room with you."

He twisted his finger through a dark strand that had escaped her bun and let his other hand wander along the edge of her breast, studying which movement made Penny's breath catch. He could easily spend hours discovering every way to make the smoky look come across her face.

Unclasping her bra, Benedict dipped his head to one perky nipple and then moved to another as he let his hands stray into her stretchy yoga pants. His hands fondled her over her cotton panties.

"Benedict…"

The low whimper was music to his ears. He doubted he'd ever tire of hearing his name on her lips as desire surged through him. "Penny," he answered as he lowered her pants and panties. God, she really was gorgeous. And his.

At least for a while.

He pushed that thought aside as his hands

roamed the perfection in his bed. He let his lips linger on her breasts before starting to move his way down her body. As he reached her midsection, Penny sat up and grabbed his face, kissing him with such passion it weakened nearly every muscle in his body.

"I want to touch you tonight." Her raspy voice echoed in the quiet room as her hands unbuttoned his pants and slid them with his boxers to the floor.

"Penny…" Before he could utter anymore, she kissed away the statement.

"Tonight I get to watch you writhe with desire. Fair is fair." Her fingers slid along his length and her eyes met his. "Find what turns you on."

Her grin was precious as she stroked him, but the answer was breathtakingly simple.

"You," Benedict murmured as her hands cupped him. "You turn me on."

Her mouth opened, forming a delicious *O* as their gazes locked.

Dipping his head, he kissed her. Not with the fire they'd had only a moment ago. But with the tender reverence calling to him. Her touch shifted from demanding to a sensation that made his heart sing.

The world shifted when Penny was with him. It felt whole, he felt whole when she was in his arms. He wasn't sure what to make of those thoughts but in this instant, he needed her in a way he'd never needed anyone else.

"Penny." Her name felt like a prayer as it hit his lips. "Penny." He dropped kisses along her chin before capturing her mouth with his, drinking her in.

"Benedict." Her tone had shifted too, but it was perfect. "I want you."

Reaching for a condom, he sheathed himself quickly. He bent his head and kissed her as he joined their bodies. She wrapped her legs around his waist, and they lost themselves in these new sensations. The new demands of their bodies.

They crested into oblivion together, and he leaned forward and kissed her forehead. There were no words for what had just occurred between them. It was simply perfection.

Her lips grazed his cheek. "Benedict." Her thumb rubbed his lower lip just before he broke the connection between them. She sighed and then looked at the clock. "I should probably get going."

He pursed his lips as he let his hand run through her dark hair. He wanted to argue. Wanted to beg her to stay. Wanted to explore whatever had just happened between them. Cling to the emotions still pooling within his soul.

But that probably wasn't a good idea. *Light*

and fluffy. The reminder did little for his heart as it hammered in his chest.

It took longer than he expected to push those feelings aside. "Just give me a minute and then I'll see you out."

She squeezed his hand and nodded.

"Penny." Benedict gripped her hand as she opened the door to leave.

Was he trying to stall her departure? She didn't want to leave but staying seemed to risk too much. Their joining had felt...different. Not like the desire from the other night, the end of a good date with a hot man. But deeper, so much deeper. And he'd felt it too... She was certain of that.

"I meant to ask this earlier, but do you want to help me with the go-fish booth at the carnival next weekend?" It seemed like such an insignificant question given whatever had just happened between them. But an easier topic to handle. So much easier.

"Of course." She dropped a chaste kiss along his jaw. "I agreed to keep things up at least until the first fundraising dinner." She swallowed and looked at him. "That's what you wanted, right?"

"Right..." Benedict nodded.

It was ridiculous, but for a moment hope had pooled in her that he might say something about tonight. That he'd brave the conversation that seemed to be hovering around them. Ask if she wanted to change the rules.

Did she want to change the rules she'd set? She didn't know. Until she had an answer, maybe it was better that they kept the rules the same. Help the hospital and enjoy each other's company for a month or so. And she'd treasure every memory.

CHAPTER SIX

"You got the go-fish station with Dr. Denbar, and I am stuck in the ring toss with Dr. Cooke." Alice rolled her eyes as she pulled her dark hair into a ponytail.

Penny wrapped her hair in a bun, mostly so there was at least a little difference between the two of them, since the day promised to be too warm to leave it down. Despite the two-year age difference, the Greene girls, as they'd been known in most of the places their parents had landed, looked so much alike that they often got asked if they were twins. A resemblance that had only solidified as they reached adulthood and the shift of their features had slowed.

"The ring toss will be fun," Penny offered as she wrapped a sparkly scrunchie around her bun. It wasn't an accessory she wore outside the hospital, but the kids at Wald Children's always responded to it. And in a children's hospital, finding joy sometimes meant looking for the small things.

"It's not the ring toss that I am complaining about. It's Dr. Cooke." Alice made a face as she clipped a smiley face barrette on the side of her head. It had been a gift from a little boy whose sister had spent nearly one hundred days in the NICU. He'd wanted his sister to always see a smiley face. So, he'd asked Alice, and she'd worn it proudly.

The little girl was now a healthy four-year-old, but they still attended many of the functions at the children's hospital. And Alice did her best to always remember to wear it. Her sister might have a tough outer shell, but she was a softy at heart.

"If I'd known I would be paired with him when I volunteered, I might have thought twice about it."

"No, you would still have volunteered." Penny hit her hip against Alice's as she picked up her lipstick.

Alice huffed before turning out the light in the bathroom and taking her leave.

"Hey!" Penny shouted as she flipped it back on. "I'm still getting ready in here!"

"The kids don't care if you're wearing lipstick." Alice stuck her head back around the doorway and waited until Penny met her gaze. "And I doubt Benedict Denbar does either."

Penny threw a washcloth at her sister as she winked. "Maybe I want to look nice for myself." She chuckled before she carefully lined her lips. It was mostly true. She did want to look nice, not for Benedict, but for herself. But if she enjoyed seeing the look of desire float over his features whenever she walked up...

Well, that was just a bonus. Her confidence was growing with each day. And with each passing day, her heart was crying out for more with Benedict.

After their rendezvous last week, something had shifted. Or at least it felt like it had. They'd shared something so much deeper than desire bubbling over. In that moment the fake relationship seemed to have slipped away, but neither of them had brought it up.

Instead it hovered in the background of everything they did. Begging to be discussed but ignored by both parties.

They'd gone to trivia night again. And won the twenty-five-dollar gift card prize for the top score. And sworn they'd make it back next week, assuming they weren't scheduled at the hospital. It was perfect...or it would be if it were real.

A real relationship with Benedict Denbar...

She swallowed as the desire pooled in her.

That was not the ground rule they'd set, and it seemed unfair to demand it now. After all, she'd been the one to set the rules. Light, fluffy, no discussion of the past. No heavy topics. No promises of anything more.

But with each passing day…

She shook her head as she looked at herself in the mirror. This feeling of wanting more, of wanting something real was just proof that she was ready for the dating world. Her heart was healed enough. She was ready for happily-ever-after.

So she'd carry on helping Benedict and Wald's raise money for the new maternity wing for as long as she needed to. By the time the fancy dinners were done, it would be perfectly fine for the illusion to end. Her heart tore a little at the thought.

Losing him completely made her want to weep. Surely they'd remain friendly. They enjoyed each other's company. Besides, men and women could be friends.

But could a man and woman who got lost in their desire for each other whenever they were alone be friends?

She clicked off the bathroom light before wandering down that path. She'd find a way to make friendship work because Benedict Denbar not being in her life wasn't an option.

* * *

Mom is not well. Her beliefs haven't changed and I'm still a disappointment. I just don't want to deal with this right now. It's been seventeen years. What's a few more months?

Benedict wanted to scream at the message. Wanted to throw his phone and pull out his hair. This was beyond ridiculous. He needed this chapter with Amber to be closed, and quickly. Thoughts of Penny crowded his brain.

He knew that their relationship wasn't meant to be forever. But he wasn't ready to say goodbye after the first fundraiser, or even after all the fundraising events were over. And it seemed unfair to her that his divorce wasn't finalized.

It had never felt bad before. His relationships were temporary, so his legal connection to Amber wasn't an issue. But with Penny…so many things felt different. He didn't want to examine those feelings, but after their night together last week, something had changed.

A seed had been planted in his soul and it bloomed whenever he was near her. Not that he'd brought it up with her.

Penny hadn't either. Part of him had hoped she would. Hoped that he wouldn't have to guess if she'd felt the dynamic alter between them.

He didn't know exactly what it meant. Marriage wasn't in his future. If the messages on his phone weren't enough proof that vows of forever were a bad idea, he still had the memories of his parents' loveless marriage and the multitude of others that followed.

And the knowledge that all their relationships started with smiles, laughter and hope. There were pictures in the old photo album of smiling faces from his father's three marriages and his mother's many more. Bright happy grins with people that they thought were forever. But the light of love always extinguished. It was simply too fickle to trust.

But Penny...

His mind twisted as her lovely face materialized. Whether Penny was interested in any kind of relationship with him beyond their arrangement made no difference. It was time to close this chapter of his life.

I need to finalize this, Amber. I am sorry, but according to my lawyer, I can move forward with the divorce without your consent given the time apart. It won't take that much time.

He hoped that was true. His lawyer had said given the length of their separation and separate lives, the court would grant the proceedings quickly, assuming Amber was ready to just sign the papers. If she wasn't, it might take more time, but he hadn't told Benedict how much more time.

He sighed and added more.

You can blame me. Tell your mother I gave you no choice. I don't mind being the bad guy here.

He was done postponing what they should have done years ago. Done living to the standard set by someone else. He hoped that Amber might find a way to find value in herself, even if her family didn't. But it wasn't his responsibility. It had never been. This was a sham, vows or not, and it needed to end.

Have you met someone?

Benedict stared at the message. It wasn't Amber's business. They'd barely been friends when they'd said *I do*. He'd promised Isiah he'd look after Amber if anything happened to him at a race, and when it had, he'd stepped in to make sure she and her baby weren't disowned by her family. If life had been fair, they'd have raised Olivia together. He'd have honored his vows and stayed beside her. But life wasn't fair. He would always mourn his brother and his tiny niece, but time moved on.

Yes.

He typed out the word and stared at it as his finger hovered over the send button. It was the truth. If Penny weren't in the picture, he'd let Amber drag this out. Let her keep up the charade so her horrid mother didn't lament her divorcée status.

Hitting Send, he waited a minute after he saw the Read status pop up. He saw the dots to say she was responding, then they disappeared. He watched them reappear and then disappear several more times.

Okay.

A few more dots appeared as she typed but no further messages came through. On Monday, he'd contact his lawyer to get the process started. Crossing his arms, he let out a sigh as a weight evaporated from his shoulders.

Happy wasn't the right emotion to describe this moment. But Benedict felt hopeful. And hopeful was a feeling he constantly told his patients' parents to hold on to. And for the first time in forever he planned to take his own advice.

His phone pinged. Benedict grabbed it from his back pocket, not really wanting to see any-

thing from Amber, but feeling obligated to follow through.

He felt his lips tip up as Penny's name topped
the message.

Alice and I are leaving in twenty minutes. Maybe
we'll be on the same metro train.

A smiley face emoji followed next.

Benedict wasn't sure what the emotions dancing through him meant. But he did know that
he'd be waiting at the Foggy Bottom metro stop
in twenty minutes. Maybe it was silly since he
and Penny would be in the booth all afternoon
together but getting extra time with the woman
was something he craved.

"Well, I think that was successful," Alice chimed
as she stepped up to the go-fish booth.

Penny handed Benedict a fishing pole before
she grabbed the box of tickets kids had passed
her all afternoon. The sun was warm, and her
cheeks felt a little burned, but the day had been
perfect. "I think so. Look at all these tickets!"

People could purchase five tickets for a dollar
or fifty for five dollars. Based on the number of
tickets in Penny and Benedict's box, the carnival
had raised a sizable amount before even counting
the money from the corporate sponsors.

"Yes." Alice waved her hand at the box of tickets. "I'm sure we raised a decent sum for the maternity wing, but I meant it was successful because Dr. Cooke got to live through the afternoon. That man is such an insufferable, whiny brat."

Benedict chuckled as he stepped next to Penny and put his arm around her waist. Penny leaned into him. The social media team had taken their picture a few times over the course of the carnival, but the camera had disappeared an hour ago.

The initial glow of the doctor and the nurse who'd helped a baby on the metro was waning. Their photos were still loaded onto the social media pages, but now there were other stories the team added too. Penny didn't mind. Particularly because Benedict's touches, like this simple one, felt so natural. Like it was just for her. No camera, no team to impress, no ulterior motive they were working toward. And she enjoyed it.

A bit too much.

"I suspect Dr. Cooke is very used to getting his way and when someone challenges that—" Benedict gestured to Alice and nodded "—he acts like a bully or a baby."

"Or both." Alice put her hands on her hips, took a deep breath, and then relaxed a bit. "On the bright side, I've got a date tonight with the photographer who was too focused on the two of you, according to Dr. Cooke. Nice guy. Bet I end up on some of those social media posts."

"You are very photogenic."

"Yes, I am, Dr. Denbar." Alice paused, holding her sister's gaze for just a moment. "Though my sister looks just as good in front of a camera. She's just less likely to step in front of it."

Benedict and Alice's banter caught Penny off guard. She felt her mouth fall open as she looked at her sister's happy face.

He squeezed Penny and kissed the top of her head before, adding, "She is something special."

"Yes. She is," Alice confirmed.

What was going on here?

Penny knew Alice had said she'd not antagonize Benedict or Penny over their... The word for whatever was going on between them failed to materialize. This didn't feel like it had a deadline anymore. But she'd been misled by her emotions before.

Still, watching Alice joke with Benedict warmed her heart. So much hope danced around her belly, mixing with the butterflies that had only intensified the closer she got to the man beside her.

"Wait, your date is tonight?" Alice's words fully registered with Penny. "I thought we were doing dinner and a movie? A nice night in."

They'd talked about it this morning. Or more

accurately, Penny had talked about it. Alice had nodded and said very little, though she hadn't actively said no to the idea. But after a long day in the sun, all Penny really wanted to do was curl up on the couch and relax.

Or curl up next to Benedict...

"Want to grab some takeout and curl up on my couch? After the long day, it sounds like a perfect way to spend the evening." Benedict's smile burned through her. "What sounds good? I can order in and have it ready for delivery by the time we get to my place."

"Are you sure? I mean, you just spent most of the day with me." Penny bit her lip and turned to check with Alice, but her sister had disappeared without a trace.

Tricky little sister!

He squeezed her hand as he held up his phone in the other hand. "I am certain. You just pick the place. There is a Thai restaurant on the corner that makes the best pad Thai. Oh, and their red curry is to die for. We could order one of each and share. Or there is a deli with sandwiches."

"Thai sounds great." Penny loved seeing him light up. So he liked spicy food, and she was going to see what kind of movie he preferred tonight. Small windows into the story that was Dr. Benedict Denbar. Maybe it was dangerous to look, and certainly dangerous to cling to small pieces of information like she'd done with Mitchel, but this was just fun.

Besides, she liked learning about the man standing before her. He was interesting and entertaining. And he lit up her insides in ways that hadn't occurred in so long. *If ever.*

After so long second-guessing herself, accepting the quiet loneliness of long distance with her ex and the added pain of rebuilding herself when her plans evaporated, the easy laughter and smiles that Benedict drew from her were a gift that Penny was going to enjoy for as long as possible.

"I have a change of clothes in my bag, in case things got off the hook here." Penny laughed. One never knew when there were so many children around if clothes would survive. Particularly when cotton candy, ice cream and finger-painting stations were involved. "I can use the locker room at the hospital to rinse the heat of the day off and meet you at your place. It did get quite hot today."

"Your nose is a little pink." Benedict ran a thumb along her jaw, and she shivered despite the heat of the day. "I have a perfectly good shower at my place. Why don't we just head there, shower and then order in."

She sucked her bottom lip in as she drank in his dark gaze. Showering here, or even returning home first, then meeting him at his place were the safer options. The ones that kept some semblance of a boundary between them. A boundary they were both failing to keep in place. She should just shower here, but her tongue refused to put those words together.

She didn't want to shower in the locker room. It was clean, but the water was never quite warm enough, and she always felt rushed. And she certainly didn't want to go home. If she went home, she'd probably lose her nerve and text him that she was tired and staying in. And suddenly dinner and movies on her couch—alone—held zero excitement.

"You sure? I can be a hot-water hog. At least according to Alice." Penny leaned her head against his shoulder, enjoying the feel of his arms as he wrapped them around her.

"We could always conserve water. Then you don't have a chance to hog it." Benedict smiled as he dropped a light kiss along her lips. His gaze burned, then shifted as he looked at her. "You got more sun than I realized. Your shoulders are burned too. I've got aloe at home. But we should get you out of the heat."

As his words dropped over her, Penny let her gaze wander to where Benedict was looking. Her shoulders were the color of strawberries. Those were going to hurt, and soon.

"What about you?" Benedict's dark skin wouldn't be as susceptible to burning but they'd been in the sun all afternoon.

"I put on a heavy SPF this morning, and I didn't choose a sleeveless top."

"It seemed like a good idea this morning with the heat." Penny pulled her backpack on and cringed as her pink shoulders rebelled against the touch. "I should have reapplied mine, but it slipped my mind."

"Give me the backpack." Benedict held out his hand. "No need for you to be super uncomfortable on the commute home."

"It's bright pink." Penny pulled it off her shoulders. Even if Benedict didn't carry it, there was no way she could let it rub against her shoulders as they walked to the metro. Just wearing it for those few moments was nearly enough to make tears appear.

"It's hard to miss the color, Penny. Let me carry it." Benedict reached for it and slung it over his shoulders, then pretended to model the accessory.

She let out a laugh at the silliness. And his sweetness. Mitchel would never have carried her bag. He'd have complained that it looked unmanly or too girlie. Or some other nonsense. But Benedict didn't look phased by the brilliant accessory.

Her heart soared at the gesture. How was she ever supposed to let him go?

She swallowed as she looped her arm through his. Light and fluffy... Enjoy the moment for what this was. She was not going to ruin it by worrying about the end. Gesturing to the exit, she smiled. "Where you go, I'll follow." The words settled in her heart as they started toward the metro. It was the phrase her parents always said to each other when transfer orders came in. Their promise that no matter where life led them, they went together. It wasn't accurate for her and Benedict.

But maybe it could be.

"Benedict?" Penny's voice carried through the shower door, and he opened it quickly. He'd said he would stick to their "conserve water" pact, even though she planned to shower in cold water to help with the heat on her shoulders. But she'd told him it wasn't necessary.

They'd had a wonderful day. When he'd mentioned how he loved picking the prizes, Penny had said she'd collect tickets and help the kids with the poles. Benedict had waited for each excited squeal as the prizes he attached to their poles rose over the board painted to look like the ocean. But behind the board, he'd been protected from the UV rays for most of the day.

And now Penny was paying the price for staying in the sun.

She was wrapped in one of his blue towels, and if her shoulders weren't the color of candy apples, he'd have pulled it off and worked his way down her body and back up again. But now wasn't the time.

"What's wrong?"

"Any chance you have a tank top I could borrow? I should have worn this shirt today and saved the sleeveless shirt for tonight, but…" She balled up the clean shirt in her hand and threw it back in her bag. "Sorry, maybe I should have headed home. I bet I won't be great company."

"You'll be you. And that means you'll be perfect." Benedict kissed her forehead. It was pink but it was her shoulders that had gotten the worst of the sun.

"You're sweet."

"I am." Benedict laughed as her mouth opened and then she giggled. "Let me grab a tank I use to work out in."

He returned less than a minute later with the white tank and handed it to her.

"Thank you." Penny sighed as she dropped the towel and slid the tank over her head. Then she pulled on a pair of shorts. Her in one of his shirts sent a pang of emotion spooling through him.

No partner had ever grabbed a shirt or pair

of boxers from his closet to just hang out in. He liked having her here, liked seeing her in his clothes. Liked the intimacy and the way she made him feel alive, really alive, for the first time in forever.

"What's Cody's Racing?"

The question rammed through his brain, driving away all the happy thoughts. He blinked and looked at her, his brain registering the shirt he'd grabbed. It had sat on the bottom of every workout drawer since he was nineteen. His reminder that he needed to do laundry. He'd been so focused on her he hadn't even noticed what he was grabbing.

He'd placed that shirt in the giveaway pile dozens of times, and always pulled it back out. Cody's Racing was the local place that had sponsored his brother's drag racing dreams... The legal ones at least. And he'd spent more days than he could count in the garage learning everything he could about engines so he could help Isiah.

He'd been there the day another kid's car had come in, so damaged that Benedict hadn't believed Cody when he said the kid had escaped alive. It was that busted wreck that had sent Benedict down the path of research to see how dangerous the sport really was.

Junior Drag Racing used slower racers, half-scale dragsters, but that didn't take out all the risk. And Isiah wasn't just racing on NHRA-approved courses. Not once he learned how much money he could make in the backwoods unregulated matches.

And when Benedict had said he wouldn't help at those races anymore... When he'd broken that vow to his brother. He swallowed as the memories threatened to overwhelm him.

"Do you want me to take the shirt off?"

"No. It's just a shirt." He hated the flinch he saw cross Penny's features.

"Don't lie to me." Penny crossed her arms. "I won't push on this, but don't lie to me."

He nodded, not trusting his ability to spill the entire truth.

"No lies." Penny kissed his cheek. "Promise?"

"Promise." Benedict let his lips wander to hers. That was an easy promise to make. He didn't want to lie to Penny. That didn't mean he was ready to spill all his secrets, but this was a vow that was easy to make.

Penny yawned as the romantic comedy credits started rolling. Tonight had been...nice. That was a word, though not an overly satisfactory one.

Her shoulders still ached. But Benedict's gentle massage with aloe and a couple of pain pills had lessened the pain significantly. By most people's definition, the night was uneventful. They'd eaten Thai, which was excellent, then popped some popcorn and started the movie. She snuggled close to him for most of the night, and he'd been careful not to jar her bright red shoulders.

If they hadn't made a fake-relationship pact a few weeks ago, this might have seemed like a lazy night between boyfriend and girlfriend. Instead…

She ran her fingers on the outline of the racing car on her shirt. She wasn't sure what it was about this shirt that had bothered Benedict so much, though whatever it was, he'd locked it away quickly. Then he'd been her normal, happy Benedict.

But she'd seen the pain. And it had called to her. But she couldn't do anything if he wouldn't talk to her. And they'd sworn to keep things light. No chance of catching feelings.

Her heart hammered, and she mentally scoffed. She'd caught feelings. *So many feelings.* She wasn't sure what she wanted to do with them yet. But she cared about Dr. Benedict Denbar, and she wasn't going to deny that truth to herself.

Her phone pinged with notifications, and Penny rolled her eyes. "I don't mind being on the hospital social media page, but there was no need for someone to tag me in the pictures."

Benedict chuckled as his lips met hers. "You're the one in most of them. I am behind the pretend ocean mostly. Except for the picture of us together at the booth. Which is an excellent photo."

"It is." That was the truth. The two of them at the beginning of the carnival. His arm wrapped around her waist and her leaning into him just slightly. The smiles on their faces were brilliant.

She looked happy. Truly happy. And she hadn't been faking the feeling, hadn't been putting on a show for the camera. She pulled her lip between her teeth. Benedict looked happy too.

What if she wanted to make this fake relationship real?

Her heart hammered as her brain played the what-if game. She was falling for him. God knew he was easy to fall for.

Mentally shaking away the question for now, Penny sat up. She didn't have to find the answers to right now. "Tonight was lovely. But I should get going before the metro stop closes." She kissed his cheek. Enjoying the pleasantness that was this simple kiss.

Movies made such a big deal out of passion. That desperate need to claim another, the feel of them deep inside you. But it was these moments she'd missed most. The easy nights, light kisses, the show of affection for affection's sake. Because you cared for the other person, not because you wanted them sexually. Rather, you simply needed them. All of them—the grumpy mornings, late-night desires and everything in between.

"Stay." Benedict's voice coated her heart.

"Stay?" Repeating the word wasn't needed, but the question escaped her lips anyway.

"Just stay with me." His fingers wrapped through hers.

Some other time would be better. Sometime when she had a change of clothes. When she had her toothbrush. When she'd thought through the thoughts rampaging across her brain. When she had a better name for whatever was happening between them.

There were dozens of reasons to say no. And if she did, Benedict would accept it. He'd offer to walk to the metro. In fact she suspected he wouldn't take no for an answer on that, considering it was after ten o'clock. But he wouldn't judge her harshly at all if she left. He'd understand.

But she didn't want to go. She wanted to be here. *With him.*

"Okay." The word spilled from her lips, and she smiled.

"You sure?" His fingers squeezed hers.

This was another shifting point. Holding his gaze, she smiled. "I'm sure."

And she was.

That was the most terrifying thing.

Terrifying...and exciting beyond all measure.

CHAPTER SEVEN

BENEDICT SMILED AS the morning light spilled across Penny's dark hair. He could count on one hand the number of women he'd let spend the night. Exactly one. And the night of simply lying next to her had brought him more fulfillment than any of the other pointless hookups he'd enjoyed in the past.

Who'd have ever thought that her sleeping in his tank top and a pair of his boxers could be so devastatingly sexy?

But with her sunburn, there would be no waking her up by trailing kisses along her body. No matter how much he yearned to. As arousal pushed through him, he kissed her forehead and slid from the bed, careful not to disturb her.

One thing that many people didn't realize was that a sunburn often drained a person's energy. In order to fix the cells damaged by the ultraviolet rays, the body activated the immune system, resulting in a general tiredness feeling the day after a significant burn. Penny needed rest.

Besides, there'd be plenty of time to kiss his way down her body later.

The thought stalled his hands as he reached for the coffee in the kitchen. What was he doing?

The scent of roasted beans filled the kitchen as he stood there. No words or thoughts coming to him.

Actually, there were thoughts.

So many of them. And all of them involved Penny.

And waking next to her often.

His hands shook as he filled a mug of coffee. He'd never had thoughts like this before. Never considered something more permanent. He'd already broken so many of the rules he'd had before Penny.

He set the mug on the counter and rolled his head, trying to gather the emotions and push them behind the walls he'd constructed. But all the feelings dancing around his head didn't vanish into the tomb he'd placed so many in. They wanted to shout with joy. Wanted to relish in the joy they brought. Wanted to claim things he had no business claiming.

He drummed his fingers along the counter for a minute, then he picked up the coffee and headed to the garage. Whenever he was overwhelmed, the garage, his tools and the ability to lose himself in a broken toy or messed-up engine calmed him.

Things that were broken were so easy to put back together. Or at least easier to return to their working condition than people. You diagnosed the issue, then replaced a wire or reattached a broken doll arm or put in a new voice box on a talking toy. It might take him a day or two to calibrate and find the right answer, but he always did.

And then the problem was fixed. The toy worked like new.

If only one could repair the human soul in such a way.

He breathed a sigh of relief as he stepped into the workshop. A broken talking robot sat on his worktable. Wald Children's had many patients that spent far too much of their childhood in the place. It did it's best to provide some of the standards of childhood. The hospital had a room full of toys for their patients and, in the case of the NICU, for their siblings to play with in the small babysitting facility while parents visited their ill babies.

And since the patients were children, toys ended up broken. *Often.* Benedict had offered to fix a toy car years ago. And then the day-care director had asked if he could look at a light-up toy that had shorted out but was one of the kids' favorites. After those two easy fixes, the director of the day care had let the other units know that he could fix almost anything.

Maybe an overstatement, but he generally found a way to get the toys operational. In the rare instances an item was damaged beyond help, he'd harvest the parts that might be used in the future and then buy a new toy for whichever unit needed it.

He could spend all morning in here. There was a talking doll that needed to be looked at too. Though the pediatric nephrologist had said if the creepy voice didn't return, the doll could just be played with as a regular doll. He understood the nephrologist's dislike of the doll. It was creepy. It was also a favorite in the nephrology department, so Benedict would do his best to get it back to its loveable creepy self.

But the robot was first up. Opening up the back cover, Benedict stared at the wires. One was frayed and disconnected. It just needed to be soldered to complete the electric connection.

It was one of the very first things he'd learned as a young boy fascinated with taking toys apart. He smiled. The very first thing he'd disassembled and attempted to put back together was a toy boom box that played a selection of kid songs. He'd managed to get it to power back on, but it never played songs again. He'd never figured out what he'd broken, no matter how long he tried.

And it had taken Isiah nearly a month to get over it. Even then he'd bring up the boom box when they were teenagers.

If he'd lived, would that have become their inside joke?

He swallowed the sad thought. Penny and Alice had little jokes. Little reminders to just themselves that they were united. The Greene Sisters. He knew they argued, all siblings did.

But Benedict and Isiah's last argument had been a big one. And Benedict had let his anger make him stay away from the drag race. He hadn't been there to inspect the car. To test the engine. To do all the things he'd promised Isiah he'd do.

"Oh, my gosh! This is amazing!" Penny held a mug of coffee and looked around the room with an awe that warmed his soul. "So this is the toy shop?"

"Toy shop?"

"Sure!" She kissed his cheek before leaning over to look at the back of the robot. "Most of the staff know very little about you, but everyone knows you run the hospital toy shop. A toy breaks and Dr. Benedict Denbar comes to the rescue."

He let his fingers wander toward hers. "I don't

like talking about the past." The words stunned him as they left his lips. He'd meant to make a joke about the toy shop. Something light and fluffy. Something that fit with them keeping each other in the dark on the important things.

"I know." Her words were so quiet as her hand slipped into his. "It's okay."

But was it?

He was so used to keeping the past buried he'd never questioned it.

Until Penny.

Dipping his lips to hers, Benedict drank in the sensations of a morning with Penny. This was a routine he'd never had. Coffee in his workshop with someone special; he could get used to this.

"Want to fix a robot?" He let go of her hand and held up a soldering unit.

Her eyes widened as she looked at the small machine. "I don't know how to use that."

"It's not hard. I can teach you. What good is a toy shop without an assistant?"

"An assistant?" Her smile brightened the whole room. "I like the sound of that."

"Me too." He grinned, matching hers, and wondered what Alice might think if she saw the two of them together now. Would she really be happy for her sister if this became something longer?

But would he be able to let Penny go if she

still really wanted the marriage and family life she'd wanted before?

He'd worry about that later. Right now he just wanted to enjoy having Penny in his shop.

"So a few things to remember." He pointed to the soldering iron, directing her attention to the heating element on the tip. "Never touch this! It heats to around four hundred degrees Celsius. We use tweezers to hold the small wires that need to be soldered back to the element."

He handed her safety goggles and felt his heart skip as she slid them on. She looked like she belonged here. With him.

Putting on his own goggles, he turned his attention to the robot, pointing to the nickel plate that had come loose from the battery, damaging the wires and creating the need for the repair. He carefully lifted the broken plate and replaced it.

"Now you're up." He flipped the switch on the soldering tool and let it heat up in its charging unit.

"I don't know. What if I break it more?" Penny looked from the tool to the toy. "The kids love these things."

"It would be nearly impossible for you to do that."

"But..."

He kissed the question away. "Then I buy the hospital a new toy robot and we harvest the parts from this one. Which is almost as fun. But you are going to do this perfectly." He grabbed a few wires from the bin where he kept the scraps and a few of the copper and nickel plates. He demonstrated how to solder the wires to the plates, then pushed a few wires toward Penny.

"Now you try."

"All right." She carefully held the iron as she bent her head and practiced on the wires. Her tongue slipped out the left side of her lips. Adorable!

She practiced a few times, then he put the robot in front of her.

She held her breath for a minute, then bent her head again, the tip of her tongue reappearing. It was picture-perfect. He'd seen others do similar things. Mary Stevens, in his high school shop class, had always clucked her tongue when soldering. And Isiah always scrunched his nose…

The memory of his brother's scrunched nose sent an unexpected wave of nostalgia. The air in the workshop vanished as memories raced through him.

Isiah bent over a workbench. Isiah laughing as Benedict tossed the tool he'd handed him back and demanded the right size of socket wrench. Isiah storming out of the garage, screaming that Benedict was jealous that he had a way out of their tiny town. A way that didn't involve college debt. He said Benedict was jealous that Isiah didn't need him.

Penny's hand slipped into his and he blinked, the memories fading into the recesses of his mind.

He'd been completely lost in the past. He reached for the walls that he always kept the past behind. But they refused to rematerialize.

"You're shaking." She flipped the soldering iron off and then put her hands on both sides of his face. "I'm here."

His heart rate slowed as he leaned his head against hers. Comfort—it was such a small thing that meant so much. "Thank you."

"Anytime." She dropped a soft kiss on his cheek. "What were you thinking about?"

"My brother. He scrunched his nose when he soldered, though he preferred for me to do all the work on the car."

"Car?" Penny picked up her coffee and took a long sip. "So you can fix cars *and* toys?"

Her tone was light, but her eyes held his. The question allowed him to expand on Isiah…or make a joke. She was giving him a choice.

He could fall so easily for her… Part of him already had. A big part.

Pushing a hand through his hair, Benedict took a deep breath. "Isiah raced for Cody's Racing on the Junior Drag Racing circuit. And I took care of his engine." The words echoed in the quiet workshop. Words he'd never spoken aloud to anyone.

"*You* took care of his engine?" Penny's head tilted. "How? You would have been a teen yourself. At least based on the little you told me about when your brother passed."

"I was seventeen when I started helping him. Cody taught me. I love tinkering with things. I started taking apart my toys not long after my sixth birthday. Putting things together, tearing them apart, seeing how they work. So they taught me, and I sat with the pit crew during the sanctioned races." His breath caught.

Closing his eyes, he let the pain wash through him. If Isiah had been happy to only do those races. If he'd never found out about the illegal races happening in the rural lands a few miles outside of their small town and the money he could win. If he'd listened to Benedict's pleas. If Benedict had gone to that last race. So many what-ifs.

What-ifs didn't get you anywhere, but banishing them seemed impossible too.

"And during the unsanctioned ones, you took care of the engine." Penny's hand squeezed his.

Of course she'd guessed. With her trivia skills, she'd know at least a little about most sports. And it wasn't a giant leap.

"Except for the last one," Benedict confirmed. "I saw a wreck the week before. The engine was pushed into the driver's compartment. The driver nearly had to have his left foot amputated."

He kept going, his soul needing to get the rest of the words out. "We argued. I told Isiah that he needed to stop the backyard races. He agreed… then changed his mind and refused to tell me why. We argued." A crack had appeared in his dam and some of his past was escaping. Though not all of it. "He told me I was jealous of the attention he was getting."

"Were you?" Penny sipped her coffee, her eyes never leaving his.

"Yes." Benedict shook his head. That was a truth that had taken him a long time to accept. He'd coveted his brother's skill, his ability to try new things, to do things without weighing the risks. But weighing the risks, understanding the odds, that was what kept you from making mistakes. *Fatal mistakes.* "Who says that about their family?"

He closed his eyes, not wanting to see her reaction to a truth he'd hidden from so many.

"Everyone, if they're honest."

His eyes shot open as she offered him a small nod. "We're all human and jealousy comes more naturally than any of us want to admit."

Penny looked at her feet as she continued,

"Alice made friends easily in every place we landed. I usually tagged along. It frustrated me to no end. I draw better than her, not that she ever practices, and am more observant. Traits she covets. Again, jealousy is natural. But so is worrying about your brother, and not wanting him to do something dangerous."

She waited a minute, then added, "And sometimes the best way that you can show love to someone is by not supporting the thing they love most if it's dangerous for them."

"Yeah. I know that."

"But you still feel responsible." Penny set her coffee mug to the side and stepped into his arms.

How had this conversation happened? They were supposed to be fixing a robot. Still, as he stroked her back, breathing in her scent, he felt close to whole for the first time in forever. "I will miss him forever. There's so much I wish I'd done differently."

Wish I'd realized that the glassiness in his eyes hid tragedy, not anger. Wish I'd paid more attention.

But he'd burdened Penny with enough of his past for today.

She squeezed him tightly, not saying anything. No platitudes, no toxic positivity statements that always seemed to make it worse, just her simple presence. It was exactly what he needed.

"Should we see if the robot works?" He winked as she looked into his eyes. Setting the robot upright, he pointed to the button.

Penny pursed her lips and pushed it. The robot lit up and started to walk across the desk. Penny clapped and bounced back and forth on her feet. "Oh! I did that. With your help, but I did it."

This was one of the things he loved about putting things back together. That feeling of accomplishment. The pleasure at seeing something broken fixed. Something made whole.

And for the first time since that awful afternoon he'd argued with Isiah, Benedict wondered if it might be possible for him to be whole again too.

"So you're going to Benedict's tonight to look at colors to paint his kitchen?" Alice handed the tablet chart to Penny.

"He just wants a little help. The whole place still has the plain cream walls it had when he moved in. Not even pictures hanging anywhere. I thought we might go to the street fair next weekend to see if we could find anything he likes. I probably won't be home tonight."

"You haven't slept in your bed all week, Penny, so I wasn't really expecting it."

"I slept there…" Penny's voice died away as her sister raised an eyebrow. She *had* been at

Benedict's place all week. It hadn't been intentional. It was just a pattern they'd slipped into after she'd helped him fix the toy robot and heard about his brother.

Another seismic shift had occurred that morning. They hadn't talked about it, but somewhere between getting stuck in the elevator, trivia dates and sunburn, their fake relationship had turned real. It was wonderful, exciting, and in that stage where one waffled between worrying the stability would fall out of it suddenly and hoping the future might be forever blissful.

And it might feel a bit more stable if she broached the topic of the shift in their relationship. But everything seemed so perfect now, and she didn't want to change anything. *Coward!*

"You're happy." Alice patted her hand. "And that makes me happy. And if he hurts you, I will make his life a living hell."

"There is no need for threats, Alice." Penny shook her head as she scrolled through the chart notes. Logan Mitchell's oxygen levels had slipped a little last night. They were still within the range considered normal, but hovering. Her stomach flipped a little as she marked a note in the chart and sent it to Dr. Cooke and Benedict. They might want to ask the pulmonologist to stop by.

"It's not a threat." Her sister winked as she grabbed another chart. "It's a promise."

"So dramatic," Penny chuckled as she started toward Logan's room.

The tiny little man was born at nearly thirty weeks. He'd overcome a serious infection and was starting to put on weight. But the oxygen rate dip concerned her.

He was sleeping and his O2 was steady but still on the low end. It might be nothing, but she'd learned long ago not to discount the tingles her intuition gave her.

"You're concerned too?" Benedict's voice was quiet, but quiet voices carried in the NICU.

"His oxygen is still within normal levels. There isn't a reason to worry." Penny said the words more to comfort herself than because they offered any true insight at the moment. "But something feels off.

"There is no fever. He's still having wet diapers, so no evidence of dehydration. But…" Penny crossed her arms as she stared at the wall of stats tracking Logan's health.

"But something feels off." Benedict nodded. "I have Dr. Huikre coming down to take a look at his lungs. He's already battled one infection. It could be another.

"I sent a message to his parents. I know Jeanne is normally here in the morning. I haven't seen

Jack recently." Benedict made a few more notes in the tablet he was carrying.

She was always impressed that he knew not only his patients, but their parents and siblings and the time when they were most likely to be able to visit. One of the sad truths of the NICU was that their babies often stayed for weeks or even months. Most parents couldn't afford to be here every minute.

"You haven't seen Jack because he's with his other fiancée or clearing out of their house since she was as shocked as I by his slimy cheating ways. Maybe the other mistress we found out about took him in." Jeanne's voice caught as she walked into the room. Her eyes were red, and she looked exhausted.

"Other fiancée… I thought…" Benedict caught the words.

They'd been engaged too. Penny had had a few conversations with her about wedding preparations. They'd pushed their date back when she'd gotten pregnant and back again when Logan was born early. Jeanne had been so hopeful he'd be able to be their little ring bearer.

"Yeah. I thought I was the only one too." Jeanne bit her lip as she stepped toward her son. "But that isn't my focus now. What is going on with Logan?"

"I'm not sure." Benedict nodded toward the

wall of information the monitors on Logan were producing.

Penny nodded at the answer. She knew parents wanted answers. Doctors and nurses wanted them too. But the truth was that sometimes they didn't know—at least not yet. And she'd seen far too many doctors who had to provide an answer, which sometimes meant changing a diagnosis if they answered too fast.

It just reinforced how suited he was to this career. Why it shouldn't matter who could help the hospital raise the most money. Dr. Benedict Denbar was the best candidate they had for the head of the department position. Though he only wanted it to ensure the maternity wing and other projects he supported had a champion.

Another reason he was perfect for it.

Jeanne slid next to her son and put her hands through the holes on the side of the crib to stroke his cheek. "So what do we do now?"

"I've ordered a consult with Dr. Huikre. She's a top-notch pediatric pulmonologist."

Benedict continued, "If there is an infection in his lungs or something else affecting them, she'll be able to determine what is happening, or if it's just a symptom of being a NICU baby hooked to monitors constantly seeing normal shifts. We'll give you a few minutes with Logan on your own. If you need anything, ring the nurses' station."

"Okay." Jeanne sucked in a breath and laid her head against the isolette. "I'll figure it out. I've messed up a lot lately, but somehow, I'll figure it out. We'll be okay."

The words weren't meant for Penny and Benedict. They'd already turned to go, but the brokenness tore through Penny. She'd felt that pain. That feeling that she'd messed up. The shame that wasn't hers but wouldn't leave her side. She paused, hesitating, then turned back around.

Jeanne's head lay against the isolette and her shoulders shook.

It wasn't her place, but she took a step forward. "Jeanne." Penny reached her hand out and stroked her shoulder.

Tears coated Jeanne's eyes as she rotated her head from looking at Logan to meeting Penny's gaze. Though Penny doubted she could clearly see her through the wall of water.

"If your fiancé hid other women from you, that is not your fault." She kept her voice low. Voices carried in the NICU, and this was not a conversation she suspected Jeanne wanted many people hearing.

"I missed so many things." She hiccupped and looked to the ceiling as she blinked back tears. "No, that isn't true. I ignored the tinges of worry because I didn't want to see what was before my eyes, particularly after I got pregnant. And he was so good at the lies, so convincing. God, I apologized for questioning him so many times."

She sucked in another breath as she turned her head to her son. "This was already so hard. I... I just wasn't prepared to do it alone."

"You aren't alone. Your sister's been here," Penny offered. "And you said your best friend has been helping you at your house. I know that may not seem like much, but when you get a chance, make a list of everyone you have in your life. I bet it's more than you think."

That was what she'd done, sitting on the floor of her apartment in Ohio. Stared at the empty picture frames, absent of her and Mitchel's smiling faces. She'd felt so stupid and alone. So lost in the world.

She'd pulled out a list and put down everyone she could call right then. And been stunned to see how many names she could add. It had lessened her burden a little in one of her darkest times.

"And *you* are not responsible for his lies. No matter how it feels right now." Penny tapped Jeanne's shoulder one last time.

She turned, surprised to see Benedict still by the doorway. She hadn't said anything about Mitchel. At least not directly, but she'd assumed Benedict had headed to another room. Stupid assumption. Unlike Dr. Cooke, Benedict always made sure his patients and their parents were as comfortable as possible in a truly uncomfortable place.

His eyes held hers for a moment before he stepped to the side and let her pass. Her stomach clinched as the memories of the past pummeled her. She'd meant everything she told Jeanne. She desperately wanted her to believe in herself. To understand that none of it was her fault...even if Penny wasn't sure she'd completely forgiven herself.

Even if she wasn't sure she'd ever fully trust her instincts again.

Benedict laid out the six different shades of blue that the woman at the hardware store swore were different colors. Laid out end to end, he could tell there were slight differences, but he couldn't imagine it making much of a difference.

But he wanted his townhome to be a home. Wanted it to be a place that Penny wanted to be, a place that was happy. Home meant security and love to Penny, and he wanted his place to mean that to her too.

Because he was falling in love with her. The emotion he never trusted, the one that had driven his parents into the arms of so many people, trying to find happiness. Love, so dangerous. And yet so impossible to avoid with Penny.

Maybe it wasn't fair to make his house feel like a home for her. He wasn't willing to walk down the aisle. To make that vow of forever. But that didn't change the feeling of completeness, the feeling that everything was right in his world that he felt each time he looked at her. Each time he touched her. Each time he thought of her.

He was falling for her...hard. Lying about it to himself wouldn't serve any purpose.

She pushed the swatches around on the counter, but he could tell she wasn't interested in the shades of blue. She'd been a shell of the woman he knew, the woman he loved, since Logan's mother arrived at the hospital. And it didn't take a giant leap for him to guess her fiancé hadn't been faithful.

They'd promised each other light and fluffy. No, she'd made that demand of their relationship, and he'd been happy with it at the time. But not anymore. He wanted to know her, really know her. To give her the comfort she'd given him so many times.

"I want to change the rules of the game." He gathered up the swatches of blue and tossed them in a drawer. They needed to talk and not about the color of the walls in his townhome. But his stomach felt dry as he prepared to finally broach the topic they'd avoided for weeks.

This wasn't fake, at least not for him, and he

didn't want to go any longer without acknowledging that.

"If you don't like blue, you could try red or some people really like yellow in the kitchen. I think it's too bright personally." She shrugged and spun the wine glass in front of her.

"Well, then yellow is definitely out." Benedict gripped her hand and let his fingers run along her palm. "Because I want this place to be a place you enjoy."

Her lips opened. "Benedict…"

She looked at him and he could see fear hovering in the blue depths, and he hated it. But there was a tinge of hope, and that was enough to keep him going. "I don't want light and fluffy, Penny. I want you and everything that comes with that."

"I don't want to get hurt again." Penny sucked in a breath. "I know life is hard and know that is such a heavy burden to lay at anyone's feet. But after Mitchel…"

She crossed her arms, and he hated the loss of her touch. The loss of the connection. He needed her. "I promised before that I wouldn't hurt you…"

"That was before we…" Penny met his gaze, then looked away.

Before they'd laughed together, before they'd slept together, before he'd fallen for her. But the promise was still one he planned to keep.

"Doesn't matter to me when it was. I meant it then, and I mean it now. I promise to do whatever I can to never hurt you." For however long these feelings lasted, Benedict would treasure her. When their feelings inevitably faded, as all feelings did, they'd find a way to part amicably without hurting the other.

"That's a giant promise." Penny kissed his cheek. "I know how important promises are to you. That one…"

"Is easily made." Benedict nodded and pulled her close, enjoying her soft sigh as she leaned her head against his shoulder. "I promise you, Penny Greene. I will do my best to never hurt you. To protect you."

To love you.

He barely caught those words. He'd do that too, but tonight wasn't the right time to make that declaration. "I don't want to put a timeline on whatever is between us, Penny. I want you in my life, but that means I'd like to know why Logan's mother's trials sent you into such a spin. You gave excellent care this afternoon, but your smiles were fake, your tone a little off."

He squeezed her tightly as he heard the soft sob she almost managed to cover. "That is not a criticism. We are entitled to off days, and no one can be perfect and happy every day. Particularly in a NICU.

"If you aren't comfortable telling me…"

"Mitchel had a family. A wife, two kids and a golden retriever." She squeezed him tightly and then stepped back. "He told his wife and me that he was traveling all the time. I was engaged for three years and the whole relationship was a lie."

She started pacing and shaking her head. "Three years, Benedict. Three whole freaking years!" She pushed her hand through her hair before hugging herself. "He was so convincing. I believed he loved me and only me, and I wanted to be settled. To have my place in the world, a place I didn't have to leave. My parents love each other, but even in retirement, the two can't stay in one place for more than three years. They love to move, but I want roots. I thought Mitchel wanted the same."

A huff echoed in the room as she looked at him but didn't quite meet his gaze. "I rescheduled my wedding twice for him. And I never questioned the reasons he gave, which were complete BS. I mean Alice could tell he was human garbage, but I wanted the home, the wedding, the kids in the suburbs."

She sucked in a deep breath as her watery gaze met his. "I wanted the fairy tale. And I silenced the tingles in the back of my brain, screaming that something was wrong."

"There is nothing wrong with wanting a fantasy. A few people even get it." Benedict stepped beside her and wiped a tear from her cheek.

Penny wiped the other tears with the back of her hand. "I know I should be glad that my parents got the happily-ever-after. That Alice and I grew up in a home with so much love. But they made it look easy. And it's just not."

"Do you still want the fantasy?" Benedict's voice was soft. "Because I didn't get to grow up with two happy parents. I grew up with a bitter, angry woman who kept hoping the next relationship would give her what the previous dozen hadn't. No promises of for better or worse were ever kept in my house."

"I want you." Penny sighed. "And I don't want to think of much more than that right now. I want to enjoy whatever we have, without any time limits. I want to know that between the two of us, this is a relationship. A real one."

"It most certainly is." He dipped his head to hers. She tasted of hope and the future. It was more than he'd allowed himself to hope for in so long. This was perfect.

Except I'm legally married.

The thought thudded through him as he held Penny tightly. Would it matter to her that he and Amber had never even kissed? That he hadn't seen her in years, and had been asking for a divorce since before he and Penny reconnected on the metro? Since she came back into town with no ring on her finger.

He didn't know. He was certain of two things. He loved Penny. And he'd promised her he'd do his best not to hurt her.

Benedict wasn't her ex. He wasn't hiding a family. He just still had an entanglement from the past. A promise to his brother—one he'd kept for too long.

He'd sworn he wouldn't hurt Penny and that vow was just as important as the promise he'd made to his brother to protect Amber if anything happened to him. Isiah, Amber and their daughter were his past. Penny was his future, and he was going to keep his promises to her.

He hadn't heard from Amber since their text exchange. His lawyer had filed the divorce paperwork and everything should be finalized shortly.

As soon as everything was done, he'd explain. When there was no chance of hurting the woman he loved.

Coward.

Benedict breathed her scent and lost himself in Penny's kisses. Everything would be all right. *It would.*

CHAPTER EIGHT

"SNICKERDOODLE COFFEE WITH just a dash of cinnamon." Benedict laid the cup in front of Penny and her whole body lit up at his smile, despite her exhaustion at the hour.

"Night shifts." Benedict winked as he raised his cup to his lips. "This rotation is always a little difficult to switch to. Have I thanked you for joining me?"

"Many times." Penny took a deep sip of her coffee, enjoying the hint of cinnamon. Dr. Kuolon had taken a position at a hospital in Texas and each of the doctors vying for Dr. Lioness's position had been assigned a few turns on the night shift.

There were always open shifts for nurses at night, so Penny had offered to switch shifts to match Benedict's. If they were on opposite shifts, the only time they'd see each other was in the brief moments where the other was barely awake as they slipped from bed or crashed into it. And she wanted more time with Benedict. It was scary to say it, but she'd never been so happy, so content. They woke together, had a quick dinner—she'd never managed to eat breakfast food at four in the afternoon. Then they'd spend an hour together, sometimes just in silence while she drew or read, and he worked with the wires or bits of electronics that seemed to accumulate in all his drawers.

People took for granted how nice it was to just exist with someone. How special it was to not *have* to carry a conversation. So often in the newness of a relationship, people talked all the time. But when the initial high wore off, could you just be with them?

She and Mitchel had never really reached that point because of the distance…and the lies between them. But with Benedict, it was different. In fact, in so many ways it felt like they'd been together forever. A few of her outfits had migrated to his closet, and he had a toothbrush at her place. Though they stayed at his place most often.

She yawned as she monitored the stats for their tiny patients at the nurses' station. The NICU was always a quiet place, but at night when the rest of the hospital was less active, it was easy to let your eyes droop while adjusting. Covering her mouth, she yawned again, then took a deep drink, enjoying the heat of the coffee and the promise of the caffeine jolt. Like many new nurses, she'd spent her first few years on night shift, and been grateful when she could move to the day shift.

"Incoming!" The call came over the radio. "Car accident sent mother into preterm labor. Baby delivered at thirty weeks at George Washington. Inbound by helicopter, ETA four minutes."

Adrenaline shot through her system rendering the coffee completely unnecessary. DC traffic was infamous, but the heli was only used for the most serious cases because with the White House less than two miles from the hospital, pilots often had to get extra clearance for takeoff.

DC was one of the few major metropolitan areas to have a medical flight team that specialized in neonates, infants and children. It was a lifesaving service provided by some truly wonderful pilots and specialists. But every time Penny saw the bright red heli in the sky, her heart sank a little.

"Ready?" Benedict asked as he slid the cell phone–looking radio into his pocket.

"As ready as possible," Penny returned. Car crashes with advanced pregnancies were unfortunately not a rare occurrence, but the range of impact it could have on the child varied from minor to tragic.

She hopped from foot to foot as the elevator rose to the rooftop exit. Her stomach slipped as the doors opened. At least Benedict was the primary physician on duty tonight, which gave the little one his or her best chance.

She looked over at him and took a deep breath. They'd handle whatever came their way tonight. Together…as a team.

The wind from the heli pushed against them as they carefully made their way to the helicopter. The pilot nodded through the glass as the flight team stepped out.

"What happened?" Benedict called over the sound of the slowing blades.

"Racers," the flight NICU nurse called back as he shifted the tiny infant in a specialty isolette to the stretcher designed to transport the machine.

"Racing?" She must have misheard. The DC streets were rarely quiet enough for that type of activity. Not that street racing should happen anywhere, but it wasn't nearly as common here as she'd seen in Ohio.

"Unfortunately," the flight nurse stated as he started to move the baby. "Two kids were racing, oblivious to the stoplight cameras that would catch everything and the lone car at the intersection. The delivery happened almost as soon as they got her to the hospital."

"Mother will be fine. Broken clavicle, a few tender ribs and a broken leg from the impact point to the right leg. With the leg injury, she won't be able to make it here for days—at least."

"But she was able to give a thorough history. Preterm contractions started after dinner. She monitored for a while, then decided to head to George Washington for observation." The paramedic shook his head and sighed. "If she'd made it to the hospital, they probably could have stopped the contractions. But…"

He shook his head and passed the papers for transport over.

Preterm labor was common enough. If she'd reached the hospital, they'd have administered a tocolytic to slow or stop the contractions. They would have then given the mother a shot of antenatal corticosteroids, commonly called ACS, to speed up the baby's lung development. Even if the tocolytic was only able to stop the labor for a few days, the ACS could help prevent a number of respiratory disasters.

"Any antibiotics administered to the mother before delivery?" Benedict's question seemed loud in the hallway after the roar of the helicopter's engines.

Penny suspected the answer, but Benedict

needed to ask. When the flight nurse shook his head, she could see that Benedict wasn't surprised either. When critical cases occurred, often there just wasn't time. But with no ACS administered and no antibiotics, the little one faced a longer battle. But it was one she and Benedict were here to ensure she won.

"What's the baby's name?" Penny looked in the transport isolette at the little one covered in sensors that she'd hook up as soon as they reached her room.

"The mother said she was supposed to be named Adeline but after what happened she decided to name her Hope."

Emotion coated the back of her throat as she looked at the little one. Her mother was scared, she'd been through an ordeal and she'd given her daughter the name she needed most. But there wasn't time to give in to the emotion now.

"It's nice to meet you, Hope." Penny stroked the edge of the isolette. It was always hard when the babies arrived without their parents. Hope's mother would not have been a candidate for the maternity ward that Benedict was arguing so hard for. But she ached for its need each time a baby landed here alone.

"Mother plans to pump but asked if there was donor milk available." The flight nurse checked a few more boxes on the tablet before handing it to Benedict to complete the official transfer of Hope's care.

"Of course." Penny was proud that Wald Children's had a bank of breast milk from mothers who had extra or who pumped extra specifically for NICU preemies. Preemies needed nutrients, but some ate as little as an ounce in each feeding. That meant one donation had the potential to do a lot of good.

In fact, many NICU graduate moms pumped and donated milk for the NICU when they got pregnant again and delivered a full-term baby. It was a nice full circle way to help other families in need.

"Good. She is beyond worried with not being able to be here. Her wife is on the West Coast for business. She said she'd take the first available flight out here, but with the three-hour difference, even taking the red-eye, she won't be here until this afternoon."

"If you see Hope's mother when you head back to George Washington, let her know that I promise to be here for her little one until her wife gets here."

It was a nice promise. But one he couldn't keep. They'd be off duty around the time the flight was taking off. Tomorrow was their day off, but he'd be dead on his feet and legally over the time where he could care for the little girl.

The flight nurse didn't say anything as he took the final notes and waved. Penny suspected that he'd heard doctors make boasts like this before. Except Benedict didn't boast. He made promises...and kept them.

As they rolled into the room that would be Hope's for the next few weeks at least, Penny looked at Benedict's shoulders. They were tight, but that could just be because of the check they had to do now.

While doing her rotations in labor and delivery, she'd been taught that there were seven main types of pregnancy injuries from car accidents, one of which had already occurred—the early birth.

Benedict slowly opened the isolette and took a penlight to look at Hope's eyes. The baby let out a soft whimper, and Penny relaxed a little.

Crying was a good sign. A silent NICU baby could spell tragedy. But preemies were sensitive to light. Still, Benedict had to check.

"I'm ordering a CT scan and an MRI. Rush."

Penny put the notes in the tablet and swallowed. "Are there broken blood vessels in her eyes?" The impact of a crash, particularly a mother being caught by the seat belt and held back, had been known to cause a contrecoup injury that mimicked shaken baby syndrome, an incredibly serious condition with lifelong consequences.

"No," Benedict stated. "But we still need to check."

She nodded and added in the additional notes. He was right, but she wasn't sure that a rush order was necessary. Still, on the night shift things seemed to move slower, so ordering it rush wasn't a terrible idea. But something about Benedict's stance worried her.

"What are you thinking?" She opened the notes section of the chart that would grow with Hope.

"That people who race cars are insane. That willfully risking your own life is bad enough but to street race with the possibility of hurting or killing an innocent..." He paused as he looked to the ceiling. "That is indefensible."

"I agree." Penny kept her words even. This was very different than what had occurred with his brother. At least she thought it was. But there were enough similarities that she understood him having issues. "But... I actually meant what do you think about Hope? Are there signs of shaken baby or some other sign of fetal trauma from the injury before she was delivered?"

"No." Benedict let out a soft sigh. "No. She looks like a thirty-week-old premature infant.

We will need to monitor her lungs more closely since she wasn't able to receive ACS in utero."

Penny added the note while he finished the final check on their newest patient. She kept her mind focused on the patient...mostly. He still wasn't relaxed, and she could see the worried energy thrumming through him.

The night passed quickly after their new arrival was settled. But the adrenaline crash sent her body straight to an exhaustion that no amount of caffeine could fully overcome. Benedict didn't seem to be coming down from the night's activities though.

He saw all his patients, did his rounds, but she saw him hovering by Hope's door. Looking over the notes he'd made in the tablet. Carefully checking the things he'd added to the notes section of Hope's chart.

He was slightly more relaxed after the mobile CT scan showed no injuries to Hope's body. But she caught him pacing until the mobile MRI confirmed that Hope hadn't suffered brain trauma.

It was good news. Hope was a thirty-week premature infant and that brought with it concerns. But babies born at the thirty-week mark had a 98 percent chance of survival. There'd be hurdles, but hurdles could be overcome.

Every NICU professional knew those odds.

So why wasn't Benedict more relaxed?

She caught another yawn as Alice walked through the front of the NICU. The next shift was here. Like most people, she looked forward to the end of a workday, but today she was beyond ready to crawl into bed and let the worry of the evening shift fall away.

She wanted to fall into bed, curl into Benedict's arm and let the shift's stresses just fall away. Life seemed simpler in Benedict's arms. She smiled, looking forward to following through with this plan.

After she'd transferred her patient files, Penny went to find Benedict. It didn't take long. He was sitting in the chair next to Hope's isolette. He looked so tired, and she ached to pull him into her arms.

"It's time to go home." Penny kept her voice low. She didn't want to startle Hope, or Benedict.

"I think I am going to stay for a while. See if Hope's other mom manages to make it." Benedict covered his mouth with the back of his hand as a yawn escaped.

She shifted on her feet and fought against the exhaustion pulling at her. "Benedict, our shift is over and even if the red-eye left right on time, she still won't be here for at least another few hours. We should go home."

"I know. Don't worry. I already clocked out." His fingers clasped hers, grounding her as he looked at her. "I just need to be here." His voice died away before his eyes met hers.

Except Penny was certain it wasn't her but someone or something from his past that he was seeing.

Before she could say anything, he rushed on, "I just want to be able to talk to her mom. Give her some of my notes."

Dr. Cooke could do that. Alice was here along with a whole suite of well-trained nurses. He didn't need to be here.

But she could see the pain echoing under the words. Bending, she kissed his head. She might not understand this need, but she wasn't going to argue. "You know you don't need to stay, right?"

"I know." He kissed her cheek. "But I need this."

"We're going to talk about it later, promise?"

His eyes wavered and she saw him process the words. This wasn't a question she was asking but a promise she was pulling from him. They'd promised this was a real relationship and that meant talking about the hard things.

Benedict pulled his keys from his pocket as he stood. He took a key from the ring and passed it over. "I'll meet you at home."

Her heart exploded at the gesture. The sign that he saw this as something long-term, as someone permanent.

The key weighed nothing…and so much as he laid it in her palm. *Home…* Until this moment she'd have said her home was the townhome she shared with Alice. She let her palm close over the key as she held his gaze. "I'll see you at home."

She tested the word. It felt right. But it wasn't his apartment—it was him. Home meant Benedict. She wasn't sure when that had happened, but it had. *Completely.*

She loved him. The truth settled deep in her as she looked at him.

He kissed her again, a light kiss, one that was friendly enough if someone walked in. But she could feel the heat there, feel the shift between them again, and she smiled. "I'll see you at home, Benedict."

Benedict… Benedict…

Isiah's voice called to him not quite close but not far away. He tried moving toward it, but his feet refused to take any of the cues he gave them.

Benedict…

Madness crept along his skin as he tried desperately to get to his brother. How long had it been since he'd heard his voice? How long since he'd seen his face?

Move.

Giving the order to his feet only served to slow them further. "Isiah!"

"Benedict!"

The voice morphed as the present wrapped its tendrils along his brain. He tried to force his feet to move once more, to reach Isiah. But the fog of the dream was already evaporating.

Penny's hands were warm on the sides of his face as he sat up, the last of the dream leaking from his brain as the on-call lounge, and the woman he loved, came fully into view.

"Benedict?" She smiled as she stroked his chin with her fingers. She looked beautiful, and rested.

Because she'd gone home, while he'd chosen the on-call suite and its uncomfortable beds designed for naps, not restful slumber.

"I'm not sure what captured you in your sleep, but…" She paused and looked at the door. "We can discuss it when we get home."

Home. He loved hearing her refer to his place as home. It lit through his soul, but part of his brain was still trapped in the past. The sound of his brother's voice refusing to relinquish its final hold on him.

"I want nothing more than to go home with you, curl up with an iced tea and watch nonsense on the bed until I fall asleep, but I need to take another quick peek at Hope's charts and check in with her mom." He sat up and stretched; his body screaming as the few hours rest on the on-call bed roosted in his bones—ever the reminder that he wasn't a twenty-something-year-old intern.

"You aren't on the clock, and her mother has already talked to Dr. Cooke. It's time to leave, Benedict."

"I won't be long."

Penny's lips tipped down, and he hated that he'd caused the frown. Hated that she'd gone home without him. Though part of him was more than a little happy that she'd come back for him. That she cared enough to see that he was okay.

That was a treasure he hadn't experienced. *Ever.*

No one looked after Benedict. His parents had always been more focused on themselves and their revolving door of partners. Amber had been understandably focused on her combined grief, and Isiah... Well, he'd been the one to look after Isiah.

"I just need to make sure..." Penny's fingers covered his lips before he could finish the sentence.

"You *just* need to come home and get some rest. Hope is doing well, her O2 levels are good and she took both her feedings this morning. There is nothing more you can add and letting yourself get exhausted won't help you, Hope or your patients on your shift tomorrow."

She pulled him to his feet and kissed his

cheek. "I know you want this position. I know you think being here more often will help, but you don't need…"

"It's not about the job." The words left his lips without warning and the look on Penny's face suggested this news didn't surprise her. Of course she would know this was more than the work. More than the hope that if he got Dr. Lioness's position, he'd be better able to advocate for the maternity unit and any other number of things that would help his patients.

This was about Isiah. About the hole that had opened in his soul so long ago.

He swallowed as her eyes held his. She paid attention to him. Noticed the changes…and cared.

There were so many words he wanted to say. So many things he should say, but his tongue felt stiff. He swallowed again, trying to will the words forward.

"Let's talk about it at home. In slippers and comfy clothes after a hot shower. Let me take care of you." She grabbed his hand and started to lead them from the on-call room.

It should have been easy to leave. Every physician cared about their patients…or at least most did. But they were taught to separate those emotions. To wall them off. It gave them a level of mental protection…ever so thin. But he needed to check on Hope.

It wasn't rational. He knew that. But it didn't change the echoes of worry tearing through him.

Car accidents, even minor ones, could spell disaster hours or even days later. And an infant, particularly a preemie, couldn't inform you of their issues. They couldn't say my head is woozy. Or I feel off. Couldn't explain the black dots floating in their eyes.

Even if he'd listened to the signs Isiah had been displaying all those years ago, Benedict wouldn't have recognized the traumatic brain injury. But if he hadn't been so angry with his brother for not listening, and for getting in a wreck—even a supposedly minor one—he would have noticed something was wrong.

Hope had been in utero when the crash had happened. He knew the images from the MRI and CT scans were clear. But drag racing teens could cause so much damage.

Penny turned as she dropped his hand and crossed her arms. She looked like she was preparing for a battle—to make him take care of himself. And she looked formidable as she raised her chin.

"She'll still be here when we're on our shifts tomorrow. Her mother has been through so much. She's splitting her time between this hospital and the one where her wife is recuperating. Give her a little space and trust the facts on this case."

That was the problem. Most of the time he didn't have an issue with reading the charts and forming an opinion based on science. But the drag racing, the car accident, the tiny baby...all of it added up to an itch his brain just couldn't quite scratch.

"And..." she hesitated before straightening her shoulders "...if you can't trust that, trust me. I checked the notes when I arrived. I was by your side last night when the MRI and CT readings came in. I am not a neonatologist, but I have worked in this area for more than a decade. Hope is doing as well as she could be. Trust me."

The intensity in her eyes shook him to his core. He let himself relax for the first time since he'd heard that street racing had caused the issue.

Could he trust her instincts?

Yes. The answer was immediate. He trusted Penny, full stop.

And she was right. He knew that. Knew that he'd done everything he could for Hope. She was at Wald Children's, one of the best hospitals in the country with a level-four NICU that was the best in the country.

He took a deep breath and looked at Penny, soaking in her simple presence. "I love you." This wasn't the right place for those words. Wasn't the best time. But they felt right as they echoed in the small on-call room.

And waiting to say them, waiting until it was the right time—whatever that meant—didn't seem nearly as important as telling her how he felt. He loved her. It was as simple as that.

"I love you too." Penny squeezed his hand. "So let's go home."

He nodded and wrapped an arm around her. "Home sounds perfect."

"The shower was one thing I needed." Benedict dropped his towel into the hamper as he looked at Penny. She was sitting crossed-legged on the bed, her legs wrapped in oversized black yoga pants and her hair in a messy bun on the top of her head.

God, she was gorgeous.

"One thing? What else did you need?" Penny's eyes glittered as they watched him advance. A small grin spread across her face as he bent his head.

He wasn't sure how he'd gone from asking her to fake a relationship to benefit the hospital to having her here all the time. But he'd never been happier. Maybe that was dangerous. If you never let yourself get too happy, to content, then you weren't surprised when life destroyed everything.

But he didn't want to think of those things now. Maybe with Penny he'd never have to consider them again. It was likely wishful thinking, but in this moment he was happy and that was all he was going to focus on.

Finally he dropped his lips to hers and felt the last twenty-four hours' trials fade away. His fingers traced the edge of her jaw as she deepened the kiss.

This was heaven. This was perfection. This was all he'd never been willing to hope for.

Penny leaned back and pulled him onto the bed.

He came willingly, letting her guide his body as she shifted and laid her head on his shoulder. The momentum had shifted from the kiss to an intimacy that felt so much deeper as her fingers ran along his chest.

"Tell me what happened. About the dream and Hope and the feelings you experienced last night." Her fingers continued to stroke his chest, but it was a peaceful connection, a beautiful reminder that after so long he wasn't alone.

"Isiah was in my dream. Or his voice was. Or at least I think it was his voice." He let out a soft sigh. "I should remember my brother's voice. Should be able to recall it, but it disappeared so many years ago. I have a general feeling, a general sense, but the actual tone... That probably sounds ridiculous."

"Not at all." Penny kissed his cheek. "I think

most people think of memory as a room full of boxes you can recall at will, but the mind doesn't work that way. It gets rid of things... even things we love and cherish, to make room for new things. It doesn't mean you didn't love your brother, that you don't still love him."

Of course she would say the perfect thing. He squeezed her shoulder and kissed her forehead. "You know he was in an accident, but his car was mostly intact. The other one lit up in flames and they had to race against the clock to get the driver out. But Isiah walked away from his. That's the crazy thing."

He looked at the ceiling as the story tumbled forth. "He was fine, at least physically, for a few hours after the crash. He and Amber were sitting on the couch, talking in low tones. He complained of a headache, but I was so angry that he'd gone to the final race and that he'd crashed."

He pushed air out of his lungs as he let the wash of memories from that fateful day rotate around his brain. Of course he could remember the painful words he'd said, the anger he'd felt, but not the sound of Isiah's voice. Not the look on his face when he grinned. Not the important things.

"Amber said something was wrong." He caught a sob in the back of his throat. "Isiah's eyes were glassy, and he was having trouble remembering the conversation they were having."

"TBI?"

"Yes," Benedict responded. "Traumatic brain injury. We thought maybe he needed sleep, so he went to take a nap. And never woke back up."

"It's why you were so concerned with Hope's MRI and CT scans." Penny let out a sigh as she grabbed one of his hands and held it in hers.

"The drag racing… I mean who street races in DC? Even at three in the morning, there are people leaving the capital, pedestrians, people just going about their lives that deserve to be able to make it home."

He sucked air into his lungs, hoping to stop the prick of tears he felt building. "Hope couldn't tell us if something was wrong. Isiah didn't have the words to describe what was happening and Amber and I didn't know."

"And your parents?"

"Stopped paying attention to the two of us when we were old enough to heat soup from the pantry in the microwave. I know that wasn't your experience, and I'm so glad it wasn't, but neither of my parents cared what was happening as long as we weren't interrupting their lives. Amber and I looked after him. She and I sat next to him in the hospital over the three days he was there."

Benedict rolled his eyes. "Though to hear my

mother tell the story, she labored by his bedside for days, praying, begging, hoping. But it was Amber and me."

"How far along was Amber's pregnancy then?" Penny yawned. "If we lie here much longer, we are going to fall asleep."

"I can think of worse things." Benedict kissed her forehead. "Not quite eight weeks. They were planning to use the money he won in the race to leave town. Her family was, is, very strict in their values."

"It must have been hard after your brother passed for her."

"Yes." Benedict swallowed the feelings those memories dredged up. "She was devastated. Then to lose Olivia. It nearly destroyed her. She's never been the same. She gave in to her mother's demands, and I've always wondered if she's punishing herself for things she couldn't control." He yawned as his body started to lose the fight against his exhaustion.

"I did my best to help. But I wasn't my brother. Wasn't the man she loved and certainly not the one she wanted."

He yawned as his eyes drooped. The night shift and lack of sleep were almost too much for him. His eyes fluttered, and he tried to push them open as Penny's voice caught his attention. "What?"

His brain was foggy but he forced himself to focus as she asked again.

"What did Amber's mother think when she found out she was pregnant? Your brother was gone."

"She told her that there was no room for an unwed mother in their family." He shook his head. "Never will understand why Amber is still so worried about her feelings."

"You're still in touch?"

The question was muffled through his fatigue. This was important. He needed to say something, but the only words that came to his tired brain were, "I love you, Penny."

CHAPTER NINE

PENNY PUT A pod in the coffee machine and tried not to grimace as the ancient machine crackled and hissed before delivering her coffee in a weak and sputtering stream. But beggars couldn't be choosers. At least this was their final night shift.

Benedict walked in the room and held up a trivia pocket notebook. "Not sure I will get any time to look at this on shift but look." He slipped the tiny book into the pocket of his scrubs. "Fits perfectly! I am going to do better the next time we head to trivia night."

"We won Tuesday night." She gripped the sides of the warm cup before taking a deep sip, hoping the caffeine would migrate directly to her bloodstream.

"No, you won." Benedict tapped the book in his pocket as he grinned. "And I love all the knowledge stored in your brain. But it would be nice to feel like more of a team player with you.

Don't want you to get embarrassed being seen with me."

He playfully winked and her heart melted. She'd never be embarrassed to be with him, but his desire to learn about something she cared about was the best gift he could have given her.

"I love playing trivia with you. Besides, I didn't know the answers to the last round of questions." Penny shrugged. "Divorce laws aren't my strong suit."

He put his own pod in the single-serve coffee maker, tapped the top of the machine and the hissing noises ceased before it delivered a strong stream of coffee. "Weird end to the night, that's true. Hopefully the announcer gets some therapy to deal with what he's going through.

"Anyway, my knowledge didn't really help the game. You had us far enough ahead that the final round didn't matter." He took a sip of his coffee, then headed to his rounds.

Penny wanted to follow, but her stomach twisted as she remembered the trivia night… and Benedict's seemingly encyclopedic knowledge of DC's divorce laws.

He was right; she'd had them far enough along that it wouldn't have mattered if they missed each of the questions in that round. But they hadn't missed them. Not a single one. Because Benedict had known every answer.

The announcer had said maybe he needed to talk to Benedict about his upcoming divorce... making it painfully obvious why the awkward subject had been chosen for the night.

It sent a ripple of concern down her spine.

Why did he know so much?

It wasn't a topic that one generally came across in trivia textbooks. Unless it was some obscure law left on the books. Like in the state of Kentucky, it's technically illegal to marry the same person four times.

She wasn't sure why that was a law. Or why the statehouse had decided it was necessary to put it on the books.

But those hadn't been the questions. Instead it had been about marital property laws in DC and how to file a case if a spouse flees to another state.

The announcer really should have called in sick to work that night.

But why had Benedict known all those answers? And why did it matter to her that he did?

He'd had a life before they'd started dating. But she remembered those early conversations in the on-call room where he'd said he had no plans to marry. He'd certainly never mentioned having been married before.

There was an easy way to find the answer. All she had to do was ask. But each time she'd started to, the words stuck in her throat. They were opening up to each other now. But there were still things that she hadn't told him. Painful pieces of her life with Mitchel that she'd never shared with anyone.

Signs she'd missed. Hunches her mind had desperately tried to warn her about. Times she'd failed to demand better answers. Rationally she knew all the blame lay with Mitchel, but there were some things she didn't want to rehash with anyone. Baggage that continued to haunt her.

Benedict had been a closed book before they started dating. It was the running joke in the office. You knew his name, knew he'd dated a good portion of the eligible women at the hospital—for short periods—knew he cared about his patients and their families, and knew he could fix toys. Outside of that, the rest of his life was a guess.

But she knew him now. *Do you?* That insidious voice haunted her.

She'd thought she'd known Mitchel. Yet he'd been able to hide a family. Hide a marriage. Hide himself.

Penny shook her head and downed the rest of her coffee. So much pain brought on by Mitchel's lies and gaslighting. He'd made her doubt herself. Made her question the love of the man she was with now.

She might not know everything about Benedict, no one could after only a few weeks of dating, but she knew he loved her. And that promises were important to him. He wouldn't hurt her. She knew that deep down.

She was just letting her past cloud the future.

Grabbing the tablet chart, she shook the final worries from her brain as she walked from the room.

At least most of them.

David Watkins lay in the oversized armchair, gentle snores echoing from him as Benedict looked at his son. Patrick had been born at thirty-four weeks. Not quite full-term, but close enough to thirty-seven weeks, which was considered full-term, that babies didn't typically land in the level-four NICU.

But his mother hadn't survived. The woman had had an undiagnosed heart condition and tragedy had struck. Then in his first twenty-four hours, Patrick's pediatrician had noticed a bluish tint and a murmur when listening to his heart. A cardiology consult had resulted in the diagnosis of pulmonary stenosis, meaning that the valve between Patrick's right ventricle and his pulmonary artery was too small.

So much to handle in a short period for David.

His son had been transported to Wald Children's two days ago and was scheduled for a balloon valvuloplasty on Friday, a procedure that would inflate the valve, letting the heart operate close to average. Though Patrick would have to see a cardiologist for the rest of his life, he'd likely have a nearly normal life.

But all that good news hadn't stopped David from worrying about his son. Which didn't surprise Benedict. Most parents, even when greeted with good news, worried about their children. His parents had been an exception, and unfortunately he knew how deep the unseen scars that parental behavior caused went.

"He's been here all day according to Alice," Penny whispered as she stepped into the room and held up her tablet chart.

"He's exhausted, but having a newborn is exhausting. Having one with a chronic heart issue—" He looked over at the sleeping man. "At least he's resting now." Benedict quietly opened the isolette to listen to Patrick's heart. He could hear the tiny murmur, but his heart rate was normal. That was good, considering his little heart was having to work harder than most.

"His O2 levels have been good all day. The cardiologist intern saw him earlier, as did Dr. McDougall. The little man is on track for his surgery," Penny recited quietly as Benedict continued his examination.

"Is everything all right?"

Benedict looked up from the baby, and saw Penny turn toward the door as the woman attached to the question entered the room.

"Patrick. Is he okay?" she repeated.

Benedict saw Penny look down at the chart. It confirmed what he already knew. Only David was listed on the child's forms. It was against the law for them to provide information without the consent of the parent.

"Sorry," Penny started, "but who are you? We only have David listed as a parent so we can't…"

"That's Daisy," David interrupted and stretched in the chair as she stood. "You can tell her anything. I'll sign whatever form. She's Patrick's…" He hesitated as he looked from his son to Daisy, tears coating his eyes,

"Aunt, I suppose. The closest thing he will have to a mother." His voice hiccupped as Daisy stepped to his side.

She put her arms around David and squeezed tightly as she looked back at Benedict. "Lori," her voice shook but she swallowed and continued, "Lori and I grew up in the same group home. We may not have been blood, but our bond was as strong as any sisters'. We swore long ago that we'd take care of each other no matter what."

She let her eyes wander to the isolette and the tips of her lips dipped as she looked at the little one. "She was so happy when she found David and so excited to give Patrick the family life we never got."

David yawned as he wiped a tear from his eye. "I don't know what I'd do right now without your support."

"And you don't have to worry about it." Daisy squeezed his shoulders again. "I'm here for you both. Always."

Benedict let out a soft sigh as he looked at the couple. So much grief. His own past sent a wave of sadness followed by the crash of hope. Patrick would be fine. Unlike Amber, David would get to take his son home. Get to watch him grow and thrive.

"Everything has just been so much lately, and I'm exhausted." He stretched, then yawned—again. "You don't realize how much more difficult things are on your own."

"You aren't alone." Daisy placed a platonic kiss on his cheek. "And I'll be able to help with more once we get hitched at city hall."

"You're getting married?" Penny covered her mouth as she looked at the couple, then at her feet.

"I know it's not traditional, but…" David pushed a hand through his hair. "Daisy, Lori and I were all close. I loved Lori, and she wanted Patrick to have the life she didn't. It was the thing she wanted most, and we… Well, we want to give him that life."

"For Lori." Daisy sighed.

"Oh," Penny stated.

Benedict saw her catch whatever words were buried in the back of her throat. It was an unusual way to handle the loss of love, but Benedict knew it wasn't that unique. His stomach twisted as he saw Penny look at the chart, trying to cover the unintentional judgment and red sheen of embarrassment crawling up her neck.

He understood. It was a lot for people to accept, but people married for all sorts of reasons. And love was only one of them. He wasn't sure it was even the most common one.

"I get talkative when I'm exhausted, clearly," David continued. "Is something wrong with Patrick? That's what we were talking about. What we should talk about."

"No," Benedict answered quickly. He knew from experience that any additional information should be passed after issuing that one single word. Parents listened for confirmation of their worst fears. Even if you had to deliver bad news, delivering it first, then waiting a minute or two before continuing was enough to help people process and hear what followed next.

"Patrick is doing great. And after his heart surgery, the little guy will spend a day or so here and then we'll be able to step him down to the level-three and then the level-two NICU. In a few years, you can send us a fifth birthday pic of him with a fun cake for our graduate wall."

"I'd like that. But with his heart..." David swallowed. "I want to be optimistic; I do. But..." he wiped away a tear "...honestly, I'm scared. There was no warning with Lori. I found her in the hall of our apartment. We saved Patrick, but she... Well it was too late for Lori." David bit his lip, and Benedict worried he was tasting blood, before continuing. "She was fine when I left for work that morning, then the whole world shifted."

"I am so sorry," Penny murmured. "But with regular cardiology checkups, there is no reason that Patrick shouldn't live a happy and normal life. He'll have to clear sports activities with his cardiologist, but it will be okay."

David nodded, then looked toward his son. Hopefully he'd start believing soon.

"That was a long night. Glad we go back to day shifts next week." She hit his hip with hers as they waited for the subway train to arrive. "I hope your promotion won't mean that for the rest of time I'll be kissing your forehead as you slip into bed and I slide out to make eggs."

He kissed her forehead. "If I get the promotion, I'll have to do a round of night shifts every few months. But I promise to be quiet as I slide into bed."

Penny's eyes brightened as the mention of the future lit across her. He lived for that sign. Lived to see her happy, to know that he'd brought that feeling. It was intoxicating.

And it was easy to talk about the future with her. Easy to see her in his future. He liked that thought.

"What do you think of Daisy and David's agreement?" Penny yawned as she stepped into the train. "Or I guess I should say, what do you think of their marriage?"

"I think whatever works for them is okay." His stomach twisted as she frowned. He'd done something similar. If Olivia had lived, he would likely still be in Oregon, working in a completely different field and married to Amber without the divorce proceeding that was working its way through the courts now. He'd have done that out of his love for Isiah because he'd promised to take care of Amber if something happened.

A promise was important. If David and Daisy felt compelled to raise Patrick together in matrimony, who was he to judge? It was honestly more sensible than marrying for love.

He loved Penny, but there were no guarantees with the emotion. If his mother made it down the aisle with her newest fiancé, it would be her sixth wedding. His father had elected to stop meeting people at the altar after his third marriage exploded. And divorce was an expensive complication. Better to love someone deeply for as long as you did and then part as amicably as possible.

"I know." Penny nodded as she gripped the handrail. "It's just such a sacrifice for both of them."

"A sacrifice for a lost love and a beloved friend."

Her eyes flashed as the words left his mouth. "Love does not obligate you to a marriage of convenience."

"It's more complicated than that." Benedict felt his nerves shiver as he tried to explain.

His divorce was nearly finalized. According to his lawyer, as soon as Amber signed the papers he'd sent via certified mail to her, the court could finalize the procedure. In DC, the case could be settled without either of them having to set foot in a courtroom since they'd been living apart for more than six months. Over sixteen years more!

It was the right decision to break his vows to her, but it had still taken years, and finding Penny, for him to feel completely okay taking the step. To accept that his promise to never be like his parents would take a hit.

"But love…"

"Is not guaranteed in marriage. It's why the

institution itself means so little." They were the wrong words. And he'd said them far too loud as he saw several heads turn his way.

Penny's face was devoid of color, and she refused to meet his gaze as she stared at her shoes.

"Penny," Benedict murmured, "I just meant it's a piece of paper. My mother has signed five marriage certificates so far. My father stopped after three. But people sign that piece of paper all the time without thinking it's forever. They take vows for a host of reasons that aren't based on the fantasy delivered in romantic comedies."

"Except real lasting love exists. People say for better or worse and mean it. I've seen it. Seen what it means for the people lucky enough to find it, and you've seen what it means for those who don't find it. What it can mean for children caught in the middle."

Except his parents had loved each of their partners once. And even though their love had failed, he'd felt hopeful when they'd each found someone else. Until the pattern of love, anger and then hate repeated itself again and again.

"You don't know that Daisy and David will have a bad marriage. Marriage for love is a modern creation. For generations people married for property, as business arrangements or because it made the most sense for their family. And they found love outside of the union." Benedict felt compelled to try to make her understand.

"Let's be honest, Benedict, we aren't really talking about Daisy and David."

And there was the truth bomb. The ticking time bomb in this perfect union. Because despite her saying she wanted fluffy and free, what Penny really wanted in life was the fairy tale. And Benedict didn't believe in the fantasy.

But he knew he loved her. And he'd promised he'd never hurt her. A promise he had every intention of keeping. He didn't know how to explain that, but he could feel the tension bubbling through them. And he knew he didn't want to lose her.

So he said the only thing that he could. "I love you." Benedict ran a hand along her cheek. If only he could stop time, he would let life freeze this moment of love before everything crashed. And he might never un-pause it, just enjoying time with Penny.

"And I love you." Penny offered him a smile, but it didn't quite reach her eyes. She reached for his free hand as she leaned against him.

To the rest of the train, it probably looked like two tired professionals in love. And they were.

But…

He buried his head in her hair, desperate to soak her up. To cling to her, to pull at the cords that suddenly looked like they might unravel if he didn't hold on.

Benedict tried to calm his racing heart. Tonight was a blip, a single issue that didn't have to mean so much. They loved each other.

We love each other.

He repeated the words to himself, desperate to calm the worry.

We love each other.

But for the first time since they'd uttered those words, Benedict worried that love wouldn't be enough.

CHAPTER TEN

"I LIKE THAT DRESS." Alice's voice caught Penny by surprise, and she barely caught the navy dress she'd been holding up in the mirror. She hadn't heard her sister come in. Though if she were honest, she'd been lost in her own thoughts.

Lost in her worries.

Since Daisy and David had told Penny and Benedict that they were planning to get married, the reins had loosened on her happiness. It was such a small moment. But she couldn't understand how Benedict could think they were doing the right thing.

No. She was putting words in his mouth, and that wasn't fair. He hadn't said that. What he'd said was he thought that getting married for love wasn't guaranteed, so it made sense to get married for other reasons. When they'd started this relationship, Penny had said she wanted light, fluffy. No strings attached.

She'd lied.

Not intentionally, and mostly to herself. She did want the fantasy. It didn't have to be soon, but what if Benedict never wanted to get married?

Did he want a family? Children? If so, would he want to marry the mother of those children? Or just live together?

Many people did that and were happy. But she always thought her life would include the promise of forever made in front of her family and friends if she fell in love again. It wasn't the marriage certificate itself, but the bond, the vow, the promise represented in taking that step.

Penny took a deep breath. Nothing in her life had seemed right since she'd discovered Mitchel's lies...until she found Benedict. But now doubt was creeping along the edges of what she'd thought she'd been so sure of.

Love. Marriage...

He'd said he didn't want the institution, that he had no intention of ever walking down the aisle. Promises were important to him, but he wouldn't vow until death do us part with someone.

Was she okay never saying I do? Okay being in love with a man who didn't want it because he thought love so fallible? Did that mean he thought their love was so shallow that it would disappear?

She wasn't ready to answer those questions... at least not yet.

"Is that for the fundraising dinner this weekend?" Alice slipped onto Penny's bed and crossed her legs.

"Yep." Penny sighed and laid the navy dress to the side as she picked up the floral one and held it up for inspection in the mirror.

She watched Alice cock her head in the reflection as she pretended to inspect the dress Penny was holding up, though she suspected her sister was scrutinizing Penny's mood. That was one good thing about practically living at Benedict's lately. She hadn't had to see Alice's inspections, answer any questions that might drive her worry higher.

But being at Benedict's no longer felt comfortable either.

There was a nervous energy humming just on the edge of their love. The sword of Damocles hanging over them. Threatening to slice the happy bubble they'd found.

She wanted to go back to the easiness they'd had before Daisy and David's revelation. The blissful knowledge that she loved him, and he loved her. The simple times of waking together, of not looking to what the future might hold, of just enjoying the present.

But eventually one had to look to the future. Didn't they?

"So what's the playboy done that's got your face so low?"

"You haven't called him a playboy lately, you know." Penny felt her lips tighten as she stared at the floral dress, then threw it aside too. That one wasn't right either.

"Well, lately I haven't seen much evidence of playboy tendencies. I haven't seen much evidence of a *fake* relationship either. I *knew* you couldn't fake a relationship to save your life. To be honest, I want credit for not gloating."

"This feels like gloating," Penny muttered just loud enough for her sister to hear.

"Maybe a little. Little sister prerogative." She winked, looking far too proud of herself. "But he makes you happy. Or at least he did. So, I say again, what happened?"

"Nothing important." That wasn't a lie. They'd had a couple announce they were getting married for the benefit of the child and his mother's wishes rather than because they loved each other. It was a major occurrence for Daisy and David but a minor thing for Penny and Benedict.

At least it should have been.

But it had raised questions. Questions about the future. Questions about her place in Benedict's life…and his in hers. Questions she didn't want to ask.

Alice stood up and marched out of the room.

Penny looked after her, but she didn't feel like chasing her sister down. At least not right now.

"Here!" Alice returned and tossed a pink dress with a slit up the hip that was sexy as hell, but the scoop neck would be acceptable for the fundraising dinner.

The dress was a contradiction, just like her and Benedict's relationship.

"Stop overthinking and put the dress on, Penny."

"I'd tell you that I wasn't overthinking—"

"But you'd be lying. Yeah, yeah, I know. Try on the dress." Her sister pointed to the outfit, then pointed at Penny. "Now."

Penny shot her sister a half-hearted glare and considered ignoring the order. But fighting with Alice was usually a losing battle. So she capitulated, stripping out of her shorts and tank top and sliding the dress over her head.

It was perfect. It hugged her curves in all the right places. The slit only hit mid-thigh. It was sexy but work-function appropriate and the color made her skin shine. She looked great, even without doing her hair. It would make Benedict's mouth water.

That thought sent a shiver of excitement through her. She could already picture the look of appreciation on his face when he saw it.

"That's the dress." Alice clapped as she moved

behind Penny, interrupting her woolgathering. "And you can pull your hair up." She twisted Penny's hair into a knot. "Now the dress is ready, the hair is planned, so all you have to do is figure out how to handle your date."

"Any recommendations?"

Alice wrapped her arms around Penny's shoulders and squeezed. "Figure out what you're willing to sacrifice for love, and what you aren't."

"And if I don't want to sacrifice anything?" Penny bit her lip as the question exited her mouth. She hadn't meant to speak. Hadn't meant to utter the words into the universe and certainly not next to her sister.

Just saying them aloud made her heart heave. Made the conversations that she and Benedict needed to have too real.

Alice leaned her head against Penny's, and she heard her sigh as her sister met her gaze in the mirror. "Love is sacrifice. Everyone gives something. If you're not willing…then…" She shrugged before sitting on the bed. "You guys going to trivia night tonight?"

"Yes." Penny nodded. That was the plan. Benedict said he wanted to see if any of the knowledge he'd gleaned from his trivia books was in the question pool tonight. *Books!* He'd read three trivia books this week. Three that he'd had her quiz him on, and he'd gotten all the questions right. Because he loved her and wanted to do things with her. That was treasure she didn't want to lose.

"Well, I hope you have fun tonight." Alice looked at her sister like there was more she wanted to say but whatever it was, Alice kept it buried. The look sent a shiver down Penny's spine, but she wasn't sure she wanted to know the rest of her sister's thoughts. At least not today.

"I have a date with a handsome spook." And just like that, her sister's playful demeanor was back. The silly Alice that didn't take anything too seriously.

"I don't think members of the intelligence community like being called spooks and there are so many around DC that it's not like they are really hiding." Penny tried to push the tension pooling in her belly away. Focusing on Alice's active and fun dating life lifted her for a moment.

Alice giggled. "That is true. This isn't even the first one I've dated, but they are more fun than politicians. And the only ones worse than politicians are politicians' sons." She playfully rolled her eyes to the ceiling. "But this is the Washington, DC, dating scene, so what is one to do?"

"Somehow you make do." Penny raised a brow as Alice hugged the doorjamb.

"I do…" She paused, and a seriousness hovered in her eyes that Penny rarely saw. "But I know what I'd sacrifice for love. And what I won't."

Then she was gone, and Penny was left staring at an empty hallway. She stood there, unable to move, unable to think...or unwilling to think. Sooty walked by the door, stopped to see that Alice wasn't in the room, then twitched his tail as he left.

That cat was never going to be her friend. But did he have to make it so personal?

And now she was thinking about a cat disliking her rather than what she should be thinking about. Penny smacked her head.

She inhaled deeply and let out a sigh. The world, and what she wanted, formed in her mind now that there was no reason for her to put off the hard thoughts beating at the invisible wall in her brain. She wanted the fairy tale. She wanted forever, marriage and hopefully a family.

She wanted the forever commitment. She wanted him to believe, really believe, that their love was forever. That saying *I do* meant *I do forever.* That love lasted without growing bitter.

She'd always understood that she wouldn't find that with Benedict...but that was before. Before their fake relationship had turned real. Before they'd said *I love you.* Those words mattered. Those words changed things. Changed lives.

* * *

Benedict looked at the clock as he waited for Penny to arrive. She'd slept at her place last night. Not a big deal, except they hadn't slept apart in weeks. They'd slept curled next to each other each night.

He yawned as he looked to the door again, knowing she wasn't there since the doorbell sensor hadn't gone off. Without her in bed next to him, he'd slept poorly. No, that was an understatement. Without Penny, he'd barely slept at all.

His brain had roamed the fretful patterns of what-if, examining the different ways their relationship had changed since Daisy and David had talked about marrying out of loyalty to their lost love. He didn't know if it was right for them, but maybe it was. Who was he to judge?

But that night shift had adjusted the perspective on his and Penny's relationship. It had raised the specter of marriage. She'd been engaged—to a man who'd lied repeatedly. A man she'd loved, at least at some point. Look at the damage he'd done.

His wife, who had loved him once, probably never believed her husband would not only cheat but put a ring on another woman's finger. That he'd promise another that he would walk down the aisle with them. What had marriage vows gotten her? Penny had actually escaped legally unscathed.

Though he knew scars to the heart cut deeper.

He had no intention of meeting anyone at the altar again. His first marriage had been for convenience, born out of a sense of obligation to Isiah. Marriage had killed his parents' happiness, turned the joy they'd once found in each other to a bitterness that led to so much damage in their family. Then they'd played that loop on repeat with other people.

People could be very happy and fulfilled without a piece of paper from the state sanctifying the union. But what if Penny needed that? He felt his brows knit.

Before he could let his mind wander that path too far, his phone pinged. His body relaxed just a little. She was here.

He pulled open the door and smiled. The world was just better when Penny was nearby. It simply was.

"Howdy, stranger."

"Howdy?" Penny raised an eyebrow. "Somehow that is not a greeting I ever expected from you." She kissed his cheek.

"Really?" He kissed her. "You do know that I am from Oregon, right? Small-town boy. Howdy is a word that's used there. At least I think so. It's been so long since I've been back."

"You ever plan to visit?" Penny asked as she took off her coat.

"No." He yawned. There was nothing left for him in Oregon. His mother only sent him news about her impending unions, for reasons he still didn't understand, and his father never reached out. Their sons were accessories to a union they'd hated.

He pushed the unhappy thoughts from his brain. The past was done, and he had no intention of reopening the wounds it offered.

"You're exhausted." She frowned.

"I missed my cuddle buddy." He wrapped his arms around her, inhaling the scent, trying to ground himself. She was here now. The uneasiness he'd felt since that night in the NICU lessened its grip on his heart as he hugged her.

He yawned again. "I'm sure I'll sleep better tonight." If she was by his side, sleep would come easily.

"I vote we stay in tonight." Penny kissed his cheek. "You're exhausted. And if I am being honest, I didn't sleep well either."

"Missed my big bed, right?" Her grin sent a thrill through him as she cocked her head.

"Maybe." She let out a sigh. "Or maybe I just missed the sexy sweetheart in the bed."

"I missed you too." He took a step back but

held on to her hands. "Maybe you could stay here…more permanently."

Penny blinked, and he held his breath as the words registered. He hadn't meant to say them, though the thought of her moving in didn't scare him at all. In fact the thought made him ecstatic.

She should be here. Should stay with him. For as long as love pulsed between them.

"That is quite a question." Penny pursed her lips as she looked at him. "I want to say yes."

"Then say yes." Benedict pulled her to him. "Say yes."

Penny put her hands on either side of his cheeks. "I love you. I'll need to talk to Alice. DC rent is expensive. I don't want to leave her without a roommate to help cover costs. But as soon as she finds one…"

"I love you." He grinned, too happy to say more. Then he let out another yawn.

"Seriously, let's stay in tonight. Order something nice and watch TV. Just relax. Let someone else have a shot at winning trivia at the bar tonight."

He wanted to argue with her. After all, he'd spent the last few weeks reading every trivia book he could easily get a hold of. There were four on hold at the library and two more that he'd downloaded on his tablet. He wanted to rule trivia with her, be the unbeatable couple so he could see her face light up with happiness. But he was exhausted.

"I think staying in might be the best idea. We can put on the channel that runs all the game shows and I can test my trivia knowledge there." He dropped a kiss to her lips, happiness building through him.

"That sounds like an excellent plan."

Benedict didn't know if there was a way to be happier. His belly was full; he'd answered five questions on the last game show they'd watched and Penny was curled in his lap. This was the definition of perfection.

"Up next, four couples try to win their dream wedding by answering trivia questions. Will love survive the heat of the question box?"

"Interesting premise for a game show." Benedict gathered the dishes from the table.

"How so?" Penny grabbed their wine glasses and followed Benedict into the kitchen.

"A game show where you win your dream wedding. How is that a prize?"

Penny's brows knitted as she set the wine glasses in front of him. "Weddings average over thirty-seven thousand dollars in DC. If you get someone else to pay for that by answering questions, why wouldn't you?"

"Thirty-seven thousand dollars, for an institution that is likely to end in divorce and unhappiness." Benedict shook his head. "Some prize." The words left his mouth before he had a chance to think them through.

"Seriously, it's a myth that most marriages end in divorce. A narrative that gets website clicks and generates ad revenue. The truth is always less interesting than a clickbait headline, but the peak for divorces was in the seventies and eighties in the US and as the average age of marriage rose, the divorce rate declined. And continues to decline." Penny raised her chin as he met her gaze.

"Marriage doesn't mean love dies. My parents were proof of that."

She was right. He knew that. But his parents…

"And my parents were proof that marriage can kill love. They've vowed forever too many, and they always end up hating their partner. At least my father gave up after his third failed marriage. My mother seems to be going for some world record of unhappy unions."

"Do you think we could end up hating each other?" Her question was barely audible, but he heard the worry echoing in it. He wanted to dismiss the fear, wanted to push it away. But he remembered his parents laughing together, remembered seeing the pictures of them together in the wedding garb, looking like the world was made for just the two of them.

And he remembered his mother telling his father she hated him. That she wished she'd never married him. And his father screaming back that she was the worst thing to ever happen to him. They'd gone from a happy, blissful young couple to bitter people who could rarely be in the same room together.

"It's hard to imagine that happening." Benedict reached for her hand, grateful when she didn't pull it away from him.

"But you can imagine it." Penny licked her lips.

"Marriage was made for practical reasons for so many years—"

"Yes, you made that argument the night that Daisy and David told us their plans and I was less impressed with the decision than you were," Penny interrupted.

"We don't have to think of this now." He ran a hand along her cheek. "Do we?"

This was a breaking point. He knew it. He knew she knew it. But somehow he hoped he could prolong what felt inevitable from happening. That they could just focus on the love they had between them now.

Two hours ago he'd asked her to move in with him. He still wanted that, but there was a look in her eyes. A look that sent a chill straight to his bones.

Penny wanted the fantasy. And he couldn't promise her that.

"Kiss me." Her words were desperate. "Kiss me, please."

Putting a hand behind her head, he drew her close dropping his lips to hers. She tasted of hope, love, but the hint of loss was already mixed in as she deepened the kiss.

"Penny." Her name echoed in his heart as it fell from his lips.

Her arms wrapped around him. "I need you." Penny trailed her lips down his jaw as her fingers trailed to the top of his pants.

Need crawled through him. He didn't want to think. Didn't want anything more than the woman here with him now. Lifting her into his arms, he carried her to his room.

Tomorrow, with its conversations, would come. But tonight he was simply here with his Penny.

His Penny...

For however long she wanted to kiss him.

CHAPTER ELEVEN

IN THE MORNING light Penny's heart felt even heavier than it had last night. Instead of having the hard conversation, she'd demanded he kiss her. Demanded he take her to bed.

And take her to bed, Benedict had. Despite their exhaustion, they'd spent most of the night making love. Making memories that she feared would have to last them.

She kissed his cheek as she slid from bed.

"Don't go." Benedict's sleepy words reverberated around her heart. There was so much behind the words, a plea for more than her to stay in bed.

She wanted to promise him she wasn't going anywhere, but the words wouldn't come, so instead she said, "Just getting coffee, sleepyhead." She kissed him again, then dropped one of his T-shirts over herself.

"Make enough for two." His tone was a little grumpy, but she was tired too. And dreading the reengagement of their conversation from last night.

She got the coffee started, and picked up her cell. They'd been so focused on each other last night that she'd forgotten to plug hers in and the charge on it was nearly gone. Benedict's phone sat next to hers.

He wasn't on call today, but she knew from experience that that didn't mean the hospital wouldn't call. She grabbed it planning to plug his in too.

The phone lit up and two messages hovered on the screen. The first was from Amber... Isiah's lost love?

Lawyer says our divorce is finalized. Thanks for everything...

She couldn't see the rest of the message, but the text for the other contact sent pain ricocheting around her.

The contact simply said *Lawyer.* The part of the message she could see read:

Divorce finalized. Please call office tomorrow...

Divorce. Benedict was divorced...officially. He'd been married to Amber, the woman he'd said was Isiah's love. Who'd been pregnant when her love died.

His understanding of Daisy and David's choice clicked into place. He'd done the same thing. Taken a chance on forever with someone out of obligation. But not out of love.

"Coffee ready?"

His chipper tone was at such odds with the feelings circulating through her. She felt confused, lost and hurt.

So hurt.

"Your divorce is finalized." The words slipped between them. She hadn't meant to say them. Hadn't meant to say anything. She handed him his phone. "And you have less than ten percent battery. You need to charge it."

She swallowed, trying to will her feet to move. To carry her away.

"Penny..."

Benedict's fingers gripped her wrists, but she felt nothing. She was numb.

"I can explain. We've been separated for seventeen years. She and Isiah were going to run away together and then..."

"And when he died, you married her because she was pregnant."

"Her mother threatened to throw her out. It may be the twenty-first century, but she is stuck in the past. Then we lost Olivia. Amber's family were all she had left then. I couldn't push for a divorce, and time just passed." He ran a hand through his hair as his dark eyes met hers.

"Did you love her?" She braced herself for the answer, whatever it was.

"No, and she didn't love me." The coffeepot dinged, and Benedict poured a cup.

He held it out to her, but she shook her head. Her hands were too shaky to hold it.

He frowned, then raised the cup to his lips. "We never even slept in the same bed."

Did he think that made it better? That marrying someone and remaining married for so long was better if you never loved them?

"If Olivia hadn't died…" She couldn't quite bring herself to finish the question.

But Benedict didn't seem to need the rest of the words. "I'd probably still be in Oregon, raising Olivia… But life took a different course. I wouldn't wish her gone, ever. But I can't reset the way my life turned out, or how it led me to you." Benedict took a step toward her, but she stepped back.

He frowned but he didn't advance any farther.

"I planned to tell you after everything was finalized. I know it may seem like Mitchel but it's different."

Her eyes met his, and she nodded. She hadn't thought of Mitchel or any of the similarities. It wasn't the lie of omission that was breaking her heart. It was knowing that he'd be willing to spend a lifetime with someone out of obligation but not risk the same thing on their love.

She crossed her arms, trying to ground herself. She was only wearing his T-shirt and a pair of panties—not exactly "storming out the door" clothing.

Why hadn't she gotten dressed this morning?

Because she hadn't wanted to leave.

"You were willing to marry someone for obligation, but the idea of marrying for love..." A sob echoed from her lips, and she gripped herself tighter. "The idea of marrying for love is too much."

"Love." Benedict set the coffee cup down, his eyes searching her face, but she couldn't meet his gaze. "Love doesn't always last."

Penny rubbed her hands along her arms, desperate for warmth as chill stole through her. "So you think what we have won't last?"

He bit his lip, and she could see the truth wrestling within him.

"I don't have the same relationship with the fantasy of happily-ever-after that you do."

"You can just say yes." Penny shook her head. And suddenly it was crystal clear what she'd sacrifice for love and what she wouldn't.

"I love you, Penny. Here and now. Isn't that enough?"

She wanted to say yes. So desperately. But she couldn't live with someone who'd look at her and think that this could be temporary. Who would always wonder if their love would cross the line to hate?

Benedict had said he wouldn't hurt her. That was a promise that had been foolish. She knew that, but she'd believed, really believed, he could find forever with her. That he could believe forever was possible.

She'd misread him, just like she'd misread Mitchel…but in such different ways. However she wasn't going to make the same mistake with Benedict that she'd made before. She wasn't waiting to see if something changed. Wasn't ignoring the red flag this time.

"No." The word was so simple and so final. "I want… I deserve to be with someone who wants to risk the hurt for the chance of finding forever."

As she walked past him, she put her hand on his shoulder. "Your parents' marriages were sad, and I am sure traumatizing, but you're using their mistakes as an excuse to not risk getting hurt." She kissed his cheek. "You stay a closed book, so you don't have to risk everything. If people don't know you, then they can't hurt you. But that is such a lonely way to lead your life."

"And using your perfect childhood as a standard is a bar too high for anyone to meet." He bowed his head and let out a soft sigh.

She knew he was hurting, but the statement cut to her core. Perhaps there was a little too much truth to it. Alice had warned her of that when she was looking at the dating apps. Rather than rise to the statement, she kissed his cheek one more time, knowing it was the last time. Hating the knowledge as her heart tore apart.

"Goodbye, Benedict."

He didn't move as she went to the room they'd shared so many times. She quickly changed and packed up the few belonging she'd accumulated over the last few weeks. When she exited, he was in the same place, the look of devastation so clear on his face.

She wanted to go to him, to hold him, to tell him it would be okay. Tell him they could figure out a way to make it right for both of them. But she'd sacrificed so much of herself for Mitchel. So much of her wants and needs. She couldn't do it again.

Penny walked past him as she exited Patrick's room. The little one had come through his heart surgery perfectly. Today he was stepping down to the less-restrictive NICU. She didn't pause, didn't do more than acknowledge his presence when work required it.

He couldn't blame her. Working with her was torture…and a blessing. The idea of not seeing her every day at least for a few hours, even with minimal contact, was too much to bear.

The last two days had nearly torn his soul apart. He'd lay in bed or pace his townhome, unable to think of anything but her. Even his workshop provided no comfort. There was simply no comfort without Penny. None.

"I can't thank you enough for the care you've given Patrick." David smiled as he looked at his son. "He looks so much like my Lori. Like a little piece of her." The words were sweet, and he didn't tear up as he said them.

"I'm sure she would be so proud of your son, and you. And glad Daisy is staying close and loving her son as she would have."

"Yes. But only as the best aunt this little guy could ever get." David stroked his son's fingers. "We decided to cancel the courthouse visit."

"Oh." Now it was his turn to be surprised by the words. They'd seemed so certain that night in the hospital.

No. They'd seemed lost in grief. Just like he and Amber had been.

He looked up at him and shrugged. "The love I had for Lori, have for Lori, I wouldn't trade that for anything. Despite the pain of raising our son alone. Daisy deserves to find that. Deserves to know the person beside her forever chose her."

"Love is risky." The words left his mouth, and he wished he could pull them back in. This wasn't the time or place for this conversation and certainly not the right person.

But David was too wrapped up with his son to notice the turmoil echoing through him—thank goodness.

"That's true." He nodded. "But love is a precious gift. Dwelling on the risk just means you lose sight of that."

Benedict swallowed the pool of emotions in his throat. The knowledge that he'd let the woman he loved walk out without trying to stop her. That he'd told her he thought their love was destined for failure…even if he hadn't said the words directly.

He carefully controlled the rampaging emotions coursing through him as he looked to the tablet chart in his hand. "The cardiologist is going to check on Patrick once he is transferred, but I meant what I said a few nights ago. Please send us photos of you and Patrick for our wall of graduates. We want to celebrate his milestones."

"Just try and stop me." David laughed, then kissed the top of his son's head. "You and me, buddy. We got this."

Benedict left the room. He wanted to talk to Penny. Needed to. He wasn't sure what the right words were or how to find them. But he needed to see her, ask her to meet him somewhere after work. Beg, if necessary.

She was standing at the nurses' station next to Alice. She turned her head away as he approached. He tried not to let that hurt. After all, he'd let her walk away.

"Can we go someplace after work to talk?" He kept his voice low, but he saw Alice's eyes widen and a soft smile spread across her face. If Penny's sister didn't think it a completely lost cause, maybe there was hope.

"There's nothing to say." Penny grabbed her tablet and the walkie-talkie they used. "Nothing."

"But what if there was?" Benedict pursed his lips. "What if I realized I made a mistake? Can we at least talk?"

Her eyes watered, and she shook herself. "No. I don't think that is a good idea. We want differ—"

"Penny, Dr. Denbar—just the people I was looking for." Susan, public relations director, smiled at them.

One of the last people Benedict wanted to see right now was the PR director. The only person he wanted to see didn't want to see him and he could barely process that information.

"The fundraiser tomorrow night; we were hoping you two might be willing to talk to the local news station. They wanted a follow-up piece. And I figured, Dr. Denbar, that you could talk about the project and the fundraising status during the evening. I know interviews aren't until next week…but you're a shoo-in for the position. May as well have people get to know you a little."

"I can't make it. Sorry." Then Penny ducked away and headed into a patient's room.

Her words didn't surprise him, and he couldn't keep the look of hurt he felt from crawling across his face. Still, he put on a smile as he looked at Susan. "I'd be happy to talk to whoever you'd like."

Her eyes tracked Penny's retreat, and he barely kept his composure as he looked at Susan and saw her register what everyone on the floor already knew. He and Penny were no longer together.

The fake relationship that had started to help raise money for the maternity wing, turned into a deep love, had broken and now lay at his feet in a pile of rubble. And he had no one to blame but himself.

"I see. Well, of course we still want you to talk. And I will find another avenue for the local news interview. Thank you, Dr. Denbar."

He nodded, not trusting his voice. He still had

six hours left on this shift. Six hours in the same
location with the woman he loved. Six hours of
hell mixed with sprinkles of heaven.

"You're really not going tonight?" Alice lay the
pink dress across the couch and crossed her
arms.

Penny set aside the book she'd been pretending
to read as she looked at her sister, ignoring the
dress she'd fantasized making Benedict's mouth
water with just a few days ago.

A lifetime ago.

"There is nothing for me at the fundraising
dinner." That wasn't true. She lived for the moments when she and Benedict were in the same
room at the hospital. Clung to the tiny clutches
of words he spoke to her.

When he'd asked her to go out after their shift,
it had taken all her willpower to stand firm. She'd
let Mitchel have chance after chance, sacrificed
her heart so many times. She wouldn't do that
again.

What if I realized I made a mistake?

Benedict's words haunted her. But she'd stood
her ground even as her heart shattered. If she
were close to him outside the office, she'd lose
herself.

"He believes that love is so temporary there is
no point in vowing forever to someone. I won't

be with someone who waits for everything to fall apart."

"That's fair."

Alice's words shook her. She'd expected her sister to argue with her. "What?"

"That's fair," she repeated. "Provided you're certain that he truly means that. That he isn't just terrified of losing you. Provided you aren't looking so hard for the fairy tale Mom and Dad had that you throw away your own."

"How is it wrong to want the fairy tale?" Penny huffed. "How is that so wrong?"

"Because, as I've told you so many times, it isn't real," Alice stated. "Mom and Dad love each other, but you act like they never fought. Like we didn't spend nearly a year in family counseling after Dad asked for an assignment at the Pentagon without talking to Mom. Their love is real, but it's not perfect. Nothing is."

"I gave Mitchel so many chances, and he didn't deserve any of them." Penny wiped at the tears streaking down her cheeks.

"Agreed. The festering wound of a man who shall not be named ever again deserved no second chances. But just make sure that Benedict doesn't deserve another chance. Or at the least that discussion he asked for. Be sure you are okay with never knowing what he meant when he said he'd made a mistake."

"Eavesdropping isn't a pretty trait, Alice." Penny glared at her sister. She didn't appreciate her sister articulating everything running through her own mind. Didn't appreciate that she was right.

Looking at the clock, Penny slipped from the chair. "Help me with my hair. And if this goes horribly wrong, I'm blaming you for all eternity."

"Fine. But if it goes right, then I get to say I told you so from here to eternity!" Alice beamed. "Dress on. Let's go!"

The fundraising event was already in full swing when Penny walked in. She looked around for Benedict but didn't see him. Her eyes roamed the faces of the men and women she worked with and the donors whom she'd never met. He had to be here somewhere.

"Thank you so much for coming, and now, ladies and gentlemen, if you'd please give your attention to Dr. Benedict Denbar, the earliest champion of this effort."

Benedict walked onto the stage and her breath caught in her throat. He looked so handsome, but she could see the pain echoing through him too. Pain that she felt so deeply too.

He cleared his throat, grabbed the microphone, then stepped to the side of the podium as a projector screen lowered from the ceiling. "Tonight

I want to tell you a little bit about myself. You see around here, I'm known as the closed book by my colleagues."

A few chuckles went up in the audience, and Penny felt her lips tip up slightly too.

Benedict nodded in acknowledgment of the chuckles, then continued, "This is my brother, Isiah." The image popping up on the screen behind him was of a boy who looked nearly identical to the man she loved, just younger. "Isiah lost his life in a racing accident while the love of his young life, Amber, was not quite eight weeks pregnant." The image of Amber holding her belly came up on the screen.

"I promised my brother that I'd take care of Amber—" the image of the two of them together, her belly slightly larger came up next "—and that meant caring for the daughter he'd never meet too."

The screen went black, and Benedict exhaled a deep sigh. "I don't have any pictures of Olivia. She lived less than twenty-four hours after being born at twenty-six weeks."

The audience let out a gasp, but Benedict kept going. "That was nearly eighteen years ago. And the survival rate for infants born at twenty-six weeks is now almost ninety percent. But not every baby is so fortunate. Amber never got to hold Olivia. She was transferred to an NICU, and we lost her." Benedict closed his eyes.

Penny started toward the front of the room. She wanted him to see her, to know that she was here. This was the most personal thing he'd ever done. Opening himself up to strangers to tell people why this was so important.

He opened his eyes, and they met hers.

She nodded and offered a small smile as a way of encouragement.

"I cannot begin to describe what that loss feels like. And I know these events are meant to be fun as we raise money for good causes, but this is so important to me. I lived it. I saw the damage. If we can keep mothers and their children together when we know the pregnancy is high-risk, we have the chance to make a real difference here. So, I hope you consider donating tonight."

He set the mic down as the room erupted in claps.

"You came." Benedict rocked on his heels as he looked at her. "You came," he repeated as his eyes raked over her.

She nodded, a host of words trapped in the back of her throat. Taking a deep breath, she reached for his hand. "That was quite the speech. Are you okay?"

"I figured it was time I stopped letting the past

drive my present. And the best way to do that is to shine a light on it, let people get to know me and look toward the future with hope instead of worry."

Penny squeezed his hand. "The mistake you realized you made?"

He shook his head. "No. Well, yes. One of the many I made. The biggest mistake was telling you I thought our love might turn to hate. Because I will love you until my last breath, Penelope Greene. I know I messed up but if you'll give me another chance—"

She put a finger over his lips. "I love you too. But I should have given you a chance the other day, should have gone for coffee or whatever you wanted to do. I let my issues with the number of chances I gave Mitchel blind me."

"I can give you the fairy tale."

She smiled at him. "I don't need the fairy tale. I need you and I want so much more. A full life, all the ups and downs and everything in between with you."

"Done." Benedict kissed her cheek.

"Dr. Denbar!" The press of people around them suddenly registered.

He held her hand and she squeezed it. "Go. Speak to the crowd. I'll be here."

"Promise?"

"Promise." Penny beamed.

He dropped a light kiss to her lips. "I love you."

"I love you too." What a thrill those words were.

"And—" he winked "—that dress makes my mouth water."

"I knew it would."

EPILOGUE

"ALL RIGHT! ALL RIGHT!" the announcer called as he rang the bell. "It's the lightning round and for this round, we're going to make it interesting."

Penny raised an eyebrow to Benedict. They'd been coming to trivia most Tuesday nights for months now and the announcer had never said anything like this. He shrugged and smiled. She still got most of the answers right, but his trivia knowledge had expanded exponentially. It was the sweetest thing anyone had ever done for her.

"Since there is no hope of beating the Donut Call List team—" he pointed to their table "—we are going to split them up and make them compete against each other for this round. What do you say, folks?"

The room sent up a cheer, and Penny looked to Benedict. "Are you okay with this?"

"Sure. It'll be fun."

"Okay, but I'm going to beat you."

Benedict leaned across the table and kissed

her nose. "Maybe, or maybe I have a surprise up my sleeve."

"Bring it!" Penny laughed.

Another buzzer was set in front of Benedict, and Penny placed her hand over hers.

"First question." The announcer looked to their table. "What month is the least popular month to get married in?"

Penny struck the bell, and Benedict laughed as she answered, "January."

"Nicely done. Second question. Why is a honeymoon called a honeymoon?"

Again, Penny struck the bell and grinned at Benedict as she answered, "Couples used to drink fermented honey during the first month of their marriage as an aphrodisiac."

"Correct."

The room cheered as another point was added to the scoreboard.

"Final question."

"You ready?" Penny beamed at Benedict as she raised her hand above her buzzer.

"Absolutely."

"Penny Greene, will you marry Benedict Denbar?"

She blinked as the words left the announcer's mouth. Her mouth fell open as Benedict slid to one knee.

"What do you say, Penny? Marry me. Make me the happiest man in the entire world."

"Yes!" she called as the room erupted in cheers. "Yes. Absolutely yes!"

"You may have won the most points, but I got the best prize." Benedict slid the ring on her finger.

"Let's call it a tie." Penny grinned as she kissed him, not caring if the moment was caught on camera phones or anything else. This was her tiny piece of perfect, and she was going to enjoy every moment of it.

"Tie it is."

* * * * *

*Look out for the next story in
the Neonatal Nurses duet*

Neonatal Doc on Her Doorstep
by Scarlet Wilson

*If you enjoyed this story, check out these
other great reads from Juliette Hyland*

**Reawakened at the South Pole
The Pediatrician's Twin Bombshell
A Stolen Kiss with the Midwife**

All available now!